Knock.

She tensed. Her eyes scanned the room. Past the stove, the shelf, the door. Then she saw it. A faint symbol, carved into the stone above the hearth. A triangle, bisected at the top. She didn't remember it being there before. It pulsed in her peripheral vision, a smudge the light didn't quite touch.

She fumbled for the recorder, pressed play without thinking.

Static. Then her own voice. But not the message she'd just recorded.

"Don't follow the footsteps."

Her heart thudded. She hadn't said that yet.

She sat up. Heart hammering now. "Hello?" she called, the word cracking in the frozen air. Nothing. Just the wind finally picking up. A low moan through the stone walls. She stood. Moved to the door.

Hand on the latch.

She told herself it could be another hiker. Maybe caught in the weather. Maybe hurt. She paused. Just long enough for doubt to root in the back of her mind. Then, another knock. This one closer. Less like someone seeking entry, more a testing knock.

She backed away. Slowly. But the recorder clicked on by itself. She hadn't touched it. It played the same message, warped slightly, repeating with mechanical detachment: "Don't follow the footsteps." Her breath caught. That voice wasn't from a past recording. It hadn't happened yet.

She turned. There, in the dust near the hearth, her boot prints. But not from tonight. A full arc looping around the room. Behind her. Silent as breath. She hadn't made those prints.

Then came a sound. Not a knock this time. A slow exhale. Wet. Ragged. As though the room itself had lungs.

Her fingers gripped the recorder, but the air turned colder.

She stepped forward, slowly. Eyes wide.

She had to open it. Curiosity would get the better of her if she didn't. Logic faded beneath that pull. Like the bothy itself needed her to witness whatever waited outside.

Her hand reached for the bolt again, slow, and uncertain, guided more by instinct than decision, as if some part of her needed to touch it, to prove the door was still real, still closed, still holding.

Behind her, the stove let out a soft hiss and went dark, the last flicker of warmth swallowed in an instant, leaving the air hollow and mean.

Then the recorder clicked, sharp and sudden, louder in the silence than it should've been.

And this time, it played her own voice, but warped, twisted, like it had been dragged through water, distance, or time:

"Don't open it."

She froze, pulse hammering in her throat, every hair on her arms rising as if the room itself had turned against her. Then came another knock, low and deliberate, as if it knew she was listening, as if it didn't need to be loud to be heard.

The latch began to rattle, not violently, but in that slow, testing way, like someone on the other side was turning it gently, over and over, waiting for her to make the mistake of helping it along.

And outside, the windows went black, it wasn't from the night, or clouds covering, but with something thicker, something that pressed against the glass like a living thing without a face.

Something deeper.

She turned away. Zipped into the sleeping bag like armour. Shoved her hands over her ears.

She didn't sleep.

Outside, the knocking continued. Slow. Patient.

The bothy breathed.

And something began to *remember* her name.

The First Arrival

Mara hated the way people looked at her in Kinlochewe. Not with pity. That, she could have managed. This was worse. Recognition tied to silence. A smile that didn't reach the eyes. She was the one who came back when her sister didn't and everyone knew it.

The guesthouse was small, clean, and utterly silent. Her boots left melting prints on the floor as she stepped inside, cradling a bag that carried more weight than it should. The woman at the desk barely looked up as Mara checked in. She didn't give her real name.

She took the key, nodded once, and climbed the narrow stairs. Her hand hovered over the doorknob for a second longer than necessary. Room four. Of course. Same number, same room, like the town wanted her to pick up exactly where she'd left off. That detail bothered her more than it should have. The room hadn't changed. Same mustard-coloured curtains, same clunky radiator.

She dropped her bag beside the bed and sat down slowly, like her body was older than it was. Thirty-five going on sixty. Or maybe grief just accelerated everything. Outside, the sky pressed low against the earth. Steel-coloured clouds hung over the hills. Rain had frozen into thin glass on the windows.

She pulled out her phone. No signal. No messages. One saved voicemail from her sister. A message from over a year ago, still not deleted. She played it on speaker.

"Hey. Still alive. The bothy's further than I thought, but I'll make it before nightfall. Don't tell Mum I'm out of reception. Love you."

The call ended in a short burst of static. Her thumb hovered over the delete button. It had hovered for months. Still, she pressed play. And still, the voice hurt like a fresh bruise.

Mara closed her eyes. She saw Sorcha's face the way it looked in old birthday photos: always a bit flushed, laughing at something off-camera. Sorcha had been softer than her, more open. Trusting of people. Trusting of the world.

And the world had eaten her alive.

She remembered one trip vividly: they were climbing the edge of the Cullins when the fog had rolled in so fast it felt like a wall. Mara had panicked. She'd pulled them back down the ridge. Sorcha had wanted to stay. "It feels alive," she'd said, almost reverently. "Like the mountain's dreaming." Mara had snapped back, cold, and sharp: "Mountains don't dream. They kill."

Sorcha had only smiled. The kind of smile that said, *but what if they do?*

The official report said missing, presumed dead. The mountain rescue team had found no trace. Not even boot prints past a certain point. As if the snow swallowed her whole. No body. No answers.

That was why Mara had come back.

Not because she believed she'd find her. But because something was wrong with the way the silence lingered. Something unfinished. There were things Sorcha knew how to do. Mark her trail, leave notes, signal for help. She wouldn't just vanish. Not like that.

Mara stood, stretched her arms until her spine cracked, and unpacked slowly. Thermals, maps, a compass she trusted more than GPS. A journal with notes. A second journal with her sister's. That one, she hesitated to open, after much deliberation and hesitation.

She opened Sorcha's journal and flipped through the entries. Some were mundane weather updates, distances, rough sketches. But others...

Mara leaned closer to one page. A strange symbol Sorcha had drawn in the margin. A triangle with a line through the top. No explanation. Just there. Repeated twice. It wasn't just a doodle. The lines were too careful. Intentional.

Mara stared at it, brow furrowed. "You weren't just hiking," she muttered.

She flipped the page, more weather notes, a hand-drawn cairn, but now everything read differently. Like she was decoding something half-buried. She scanned more pages. Mentions of cairns, standing stones, phrases like "the old path" and "the watcher at dusk."

Was she just being poetic? Or was she looking for something?

Eventually, hunger pushed her downstairs. The pub across the road looked half-dead. Lights on, but no movement behind the frosted windows. She crossed over anyway. The door creaked when she pushed it. Inside: warmth, the smell of old beer and peat smoke, and five sets of eyes turning toward her. Older men. One woman behind the bar. All locals. No one said anything.

She nodded once. Walked to the bar. "Whisky. Whatever's peated." The woman poured a Bowmore without a word. Mara took her glass and sat in the far corner. No one approached her. But she heard a whisper. Low, from the end of the bar.

"That's the sister, aye?"

She didn't acknowledge them.

"Came back after all this time."

She didn't need to look to know they'd turned away when she glanced up. She wasn't a person to them. She was a story they wished had stayed finished.

But one man at the bar kept watching. Older, in his sixties, red thread veins in his cheeks. A slow drinker.

He finally muttered, just loud enough for her to hear: "Not the first time someone's gone missing up there."

Mara looked at him. His eyes didn't flinch.

He went on, slow and low. "They say the glen keeps what it likes. Same as it always has."

Another man elbowed him sharply. "That's enough, Iain."

The old man nodded, finished his drink, and stood. As he passed Mara's table, he paused.

"If you go," he said, "don't follow anything that walks like it's human. Not after sundown."

Then he left.

Mara watched the door swing shut, the brass handle still quivering from his exit. His words stuck in her chest like a splinter. It wasn't just a warning, a regret.

Sorcha would've followed. Of course she would've. She'd always looked for the magic in the mundane, even when the world said not to. A thin silence fell over the bar, the kind that made the atmosphere feel suddenly heavy. For a heartbeat she considered calling him back, asking what it was he'd really seen in the hills.

Instead she lifted her glass, took a slow measured sip, and let the whisky burn a path to her stomach. "Not after sundown," she echoed under her breath, half-scoffing, half-memorising. The amber liquid steadied her hands but not the prickle at the base of her neck.

Only when she set the glass down did she notice the other patrons pointedly avoiding her gaze, as if the warning had brushed against all of them. The barmaid offered a tight, apologetic smile that said: "we've all heard stories, but we don't repeat them out loud."

Mara exhaled through her nose, shoved a damp strand of hair behind her ear, and forced a small, defiant nod to no one in particular. "Right then," she murmured, pushing the empty glass forward for another pour. "Here's to shadows you don't chase."

Mara drank slowly. Let the whisky burn her throat clean. When she finished, she set the glass down and left without a word. The cold punched her lungs when she stepped back outside. Back in her room, she turned the radiator up and lay on the bed without undressing. Eyes open. Listening to nothing. The land outside felt alive, not in a comforting way. In the way of things watching from just behind the tree line. In the way grief hollowed you out until the quiet echoed inside your chest.

Tomorrow, she'd go into the hills. Tomorrow, she'd walk the last path her sister ever took. And maybe. Just maybe. Someone would answer.

The morning came in slow and grey, the kind that didn't really rise so much as reveal itself. Mara hadn't slept much. She stepped outside before the shops opened, boots crunching softly on the frost-laced road. The town looked exactly as it had the day they called off the search. A still-life of grief painted over with normalcy. A pub window still had last year's Hogmanay sign taped up. A church bell didn't ring. She passed a noticeboard with a faded missing persons flyer curling at the edges. Not Sorcha. A man. Different year. No one had taken it down.

She didn't stop walking until she reached the trailhead sign. Just to see it. Just to remember where the search had started and ended. The wood was damp. Moss curled along the base. Someone had scratched over the trail name with a jagged mark. She touched it, briefly, then turned back toward the village.

The shop hadn't changed. Same creaky floorboards, same faint smell of dust and gas canisters. The shelves were stocked with just enough of everything. Porridge packets, hiking fuel, midge repellent, first aid kits in plastic boxes. A tourist might call it charming. Mara didn't feel charmed. Behind the counter stood the same man who'd sold Sorcha her supplies the year before. She remembered his face from the CCTV footage the police pulled, grainy and pale, handing over a bundle of waterproofs and energy bars. He glanced up as she entered, eyes narrowing with the same recognition she'd grown to hate.

"You're back," he said. Not a question.

Mara nodded once. "Just need a few things."

He didn't move. "You were here when they searched."

"I was."

He scratched the side of his nose, looked like he wanted to say more. Then thought better of it.

She walked the aisles with her basket, picking up what she needed: a camping stove, matches, oats, a fresh compass just in case. She knew better than to rely on electronics out there. The Highlands didn't care about your battery life.

From the counter, the man finally spoke again. "You know the bothy's still there. But it's not been right. Not since."

Mara looked up. "Not right how?"

He shrugged. "I don't go up. Haven't for years. Heard things, though. Folk say it feels… off. Like being watched. One lad said he heard someone walking the floor above him all night. But the bothy doesn't *have* a second floor."

"Search team came back empty, twice," he added. "Locals don't go past the burn anymore. Few who did… well. They either don't talk about it or don't come back. Easy to let things fade when no one asks the right questions."

Mara said nothing. She didn't believe in ghosts. But she didn't believe in perfect disappearances either.

The man leaned in slightly, lowering his voice. "If you find anything. Anything that don't belong. Don't touch it. The land takes what's stolen. Always has."

Mara blinked. "What does that mean?"

He scratched his cheek, looked like he regretted saying anything.

"Old tale. From before the clearances. They used to say the glen had a spirit. A watcher. Not a ghost, A… A memory, given form. It guards the old ways. Cairns. Stones. The paths no one maps. If you take something without asking, it follows… always."

Mara tried to laugh but couldn't. "And the symbols?"

"Markers. Some say they show what's been claimed already. Others say they're warnings. But no one agrees on what they mean anymore. That's the problem with old things. They outlive the words we used for them."

She stared at him. "What did you say?"

He paused. Then gave a tight smile. "Sorry. Old stories. Don't mind me."

Mara paid in silence, packed her things with mechanical efficiency, and stepped back out into the cold. Outside, the wind had picked up.

She found herself standing near the trail marker just outside of town. A simple wooden post with a faded symbol carved into it, marking the start of the path toward Shena Vall.

From here, the mountains loomed like dark gods, hunched and waiting. White capped, silent. There were no fences, no gates, nothing to stop her. Just open land and the long, unkind miles ahead. She took out her journal and flipped through the pages, rough maps, handwritten notes, photocopies from the search files. Sorcha's last confirmed location. Weather reports. Everything she could get her hands on. And then there was the note Sorcha had left in their shared folder before the trip.

A half-finished itinerary. She'd typed: *"Day 3: Shena Vall bothy. Should be quiet this time of year. Can't wait. Feels ancient out there. Wild. Like the bones of the earth are still close to the surface."*

That was Sorcha. Always chasing places that felt older than people. She'd said once that the Highlands felt more alive than the cities, like the land had moods. Mara had laughed then.

She wasn't laughing now.

She closed the notebook and walked to the edge of the trail, staring down the path that led between the hills. The wind howled once, hard, and cold enough to sting her cheeks. She pulled her scarf tighter.

Back at the guesthouse, she laid her gear out on the bed one last time: food, thermal gear, satellite phone, compass, fuel, knife, torch, journal. No talismans. No lucky charms. That night she slept lightly, the kind of sleep that never sank deep enough to rest. Every creak of the radiator, every rattle of wind on the glass made her jolt awake. At 4:37 a.m., she gave up. Packed her bag. Made tea she didn't drink. Then she left before the sun rose.

At the edge of town, she passed a man walking his dog. He looked at her, paused, and said quietly, "Don't stay past dark."

She stopped. "What did you say?"

He shook his head. "Nothing. Good luck." Mara watched him disappear down the frost-lined road, then turned toward the trail again.

Tomorrow was for ghosts.

Today was for answers.

She walked until the houses thinned to stone walls and sleeping sheep. The sky bruised purple above the hills, and frost rimmed the grass in brittle lace. The trail marker stood just ahead.

Weather-worn wood marked with an almost-faded symbol, a shape that looked like a triangle cut through the top.

She paused.

The wind had died here. It was too quiet.

Her boots crunched softly on the frost. One step. Then another. But the third step didn't sound right. Not a crunch. Something softer. A muffled resistance beneath her foot. She looked down. No snow.

Just black earth.

Soft.

She lifted her boot and saw it had sunk slightly, as if the ground had breathed in beneath her.

She glanced behind.

The man with the dog was long gone. So was the town. The trail stretched ahead, narrow and pale, into the waiting hush of the hills.

She crossed a low stile and stepped into something colder than wind.

By the time Mara reached the ridgeline, the wind had found its voice again. It screamed over the moors in long, ragged bursts, dragging stinging flakes sideways across the slope. Her hood snapped against her ears. Every step was a fight, not against exhaustion, not yet, but against the land's quiet refusal to be crossed.

She was four hours in.

The trail had vanished somewhere past Lochan Fada. Buried under thin layers of snow that hid the path, then the stones, then everything. What was left was instinct and the map, but even the map felt out of date, like the hills had rearranged themselves when no one was watching.

She stopped to rest behind a rock shelf, shielding herself from the wind. Her legs ached. Her hands burned from the cold, even in thick gloves. She took out her flask, drank half-melted tea that tasted of metal, and tried not to think about the last time this route had been walked.

Sorcha had been here.

Somewhere along this same stretch. Alone. Tired, probably. Maybe humming to herself like she used to when she hiked. Maybe watching the clouds break over the peaks and thinking she was safe. That the hills were just hills.

Mara stood again. Her breath steamed around her face, swallowed quickly by the wind.

She pressed on.

The land got quieter the deeper she went. Not in volume, the wind never stopped, but in presence. No birds. No deer. No sound except what she made. The rhythm of her boots, the crunch of frost, the occasional shifting of her pack. And underneath that, something else.

Something *off*.

She didn't believe in hauntings. But she couldn't explain the sensation that kept returning, like walking into a room just after someone left. The air disturbed. The atmosphere pulled taut. By midday, the bothy emerged from the valley's curve, a low, slouched shape of slate and shadow. Its door hung half-open, swaying in a wind that hadn't moved until now.

Mara stopped.

She raised her phone, snapped a photo, and winced. The image looked distorted. Too sharp at the edges. Like it had caught something real the eye wasn't meant to see.

She looked again at the bothy. It hadn't moved, but something about it felt... poised. Like an animal waiting to spring, though nothing stirred.

She reached into her jacket for the old map the man had given her. Unfolded it slowly. Her fingers trembled. Not from cold, but something deeper, a hum in the air that made her teeth ache. The paper smelled like mildew and woodsmoke. One path was marked faintly in pencil, looping toward the bothy before disappearing behind a hand-drawn symbol. A spiral. She traced it with her glove.

It looked like the one she'd seen scratched into the tree.

The wind picked up, cold and deliberate, pushing against her back. Not hard, but insistent. She stepped forward without thinking, boots crunching on the frost-hardened ground. Each step felt louder than it should have.

When she reached the door, it moved slightly. Just a creak. But it hadn't been touched. She paused, staring at it.

From inside: nothing.

But as she stood at the threshold, she thought. No, *felt*. Someone watching her. Not with malice. With memory. Like the building knew her already.

She approached slowly, boots crunching louder now, as if the snow were trying to warn her. She reached the door. Paused. Pushed it open.

Inside: dark.

Not pitch black. The slatted window let in some dim light, but shadowed and cold. The air smelled of old peat, damp stone, and something faintly sour. Not rot. Just... left behind.

She stepped in, let the door creak shut behind her.

Inside: a single room. One bench. A rusted stove. A few dusty tins on a crooked shelf. Someone had carved "Leave no trace" into the wood above the hearth. Beneath it, another hand had added: "Too late."

Mara dropped her pack. Her fingers trembled. The cold, maybe. Or not.

She lit her stove. The flame flickered weakly, shadows shivering up the walls like they were trying to climb out.

She took out her notebook. Skimmed Sorcha's last entry again. Her fingers paused on a line she'd read a dozen times.

"Knocking outside the bothy. Can't tell if it's wind or not. Gave me the creeps."

She looked at the door.

Nothing.

No wind, either. Not inside. The bothy held its breath. Mara forced herself to eat. Instant noodles. Her stomach wasn't interested, but her body needed the warmth.

She checked the walls for any signs. Carvings, messages, anything Sorcha might have left. Nothing.

But the air felt heavier now. Like being underwater.

She took out the old recorder. Sorcha's.

It still worked. She pressed play, just to see if there was anything left. Static. Then a faint voice: *"I don't think I'm alone here."*

A pause. Then: *"It knocks three times."*

Mara stopped the tape. She sat frozen, pulse in her ears.

Suddenly. From outside.

Knock.

She turned toward the door.

Knock.

Not hard. Not frantic. Just deliberate.

Knock.

Three times.

Then silence.

Mara stood very still.

The wind had stopped again.

And the bothy was breathing.

The Return

The bridge into Kinlochewe was narrow. One car at a time, flanked by iron rails rusting under years of Highland rain. Mara crossed it slowly, pack heavy on her shoulders, boots already wet from a failed detour through the boggy edge of the loch.

The cold wasn't sharp, but it was constant. Settled in her gloves, her spine, the back of her neck. It made everything feel harder, not dangerous, just resistant. As if the land didn't want her moving forward.

She stepped onto firmer gravel and paused to catch her breath.

That's when she saw him.

The old man stood a few yards ahead, facing the river. Bent slightly, hands folded over the top of a worn walking stick. His coat looked older than her, thick wool patched at the elbows. His hair was white, tangled under a knit cap. He hadn't turned at the sound of her boots.

"Morning," Mara said, stepping past.

"That's a heavy pack for one night," he said, still facing the river.

She stopped. "I'm not camping," she replied. "Just heading into the hills." He turned then. Slowly. Looked her full in the face. His eyes were pale grey, with the watery, film-like sheen of someone long past caring about what he saw. But they were focused.

"You're the sister," he said. Mara didn't answer. He nodded to himself. "Thought so. You've got the same walk. Shoulders pulled in, like you expect the cold to do worse than freeze you."

She adjusted the strap on her pack. "Have we met?"

He didn't answer right away. Instead, he took a slow step forward and said, "You know what the old people called this land?"

She stayed silent.

"An Dùthaich Ghluasadach. The shifting land."

"The kind of place where a hill might be taller tomorrow. Or a path shorter than you remembered. Or longer."

"They said the earth out here has moods."

"I'm not out here for stories."

"Aye. You're out here for the girl."

The way he said it. Not your sister, not Sorcha. Made something tighten in Mara's throat.

He went on. "The hills keep what they take. And they took her quiet, didn't they? Not a scream, not a struggle. Just gone."

"She's not..." Mara started, but the word dead refused to leave her mouth.

The old man nodded slowly. "You've already heard it, haven't you? The knocking?"

She froze.

His lips thinned into something that wasn't quite a smile. "Everyone hears it. Not always outside, though. Sometimes it's inside the walls. Sometimes... it's in the ground."

"You don't know anything about her," Mara said. "Or me."

He didn't argue.

He just said, "Don't stay past the second night. Whatever you're looking for, it won't be there after that."

She took a step back. "Thanks for the advice."

The old man turned away again, back to the river. "There are stories we used to tell," he said. "Then we stopped. Not because they weren't true. But because they were."

Mara walked away before he could say anything else. The shop was quiet again. Same man behind the counter, though this time he didn't speak when she walked in. Just nodded.

She moved efficiently. Fuel, food, water filter. She hesitated at the shelf of personal locator beacons, a safety net for solo hikers. After a pause, she picked one up and added it to her pile.

"Smart," the man said as she brought her things to the counter. "Folk think they don't need one, then go missing under blue skies." Mara said nothing.

He looked at the beacon again, just a beat too long.

"Used to go up there myself. Not anymore," he said, voice low. "My brother never came back from Beinn Eighe. 1997. Folks say he wandered too far. But he knew those trails better than most."

Mara paused. "I'm sorry."

He nodded once. "I was the one who told him to take the bothy route. Safer, I said. Warmer. Thought it'd save him."

He met her eyes then, and in his expression was the same thing she saw in her own: the ache of a story that kept rewriting itself.

He looked at her for a moment, then reached under the counter and pulled out a folded paper. "Trail notes," he said. "Someone local updated the route markings last month. You'll want this, snow's come in heavier than usual."

She took it. "Thanks."

"You going far?"

"Shena Vall," she said.

His eyes didn't change, but his mouth thinned slightly. "Weather's not friendly."

"I'm not expecting it to be."

She left the shop before he could say anything else.

Back at the guesthouse, she packed everything with clinical precision. She didn't check her phone, no one had messaged anyway. She laid out Sorcha's journal one last time, rereading that final entry. The one that mentioned the bothy. The one that ended mid-sentence.

That night, the wind woke her twice.

And at 3:14 a.m., she thought she heard something knock once. Far off, like a boot against wood. Before silence took it back.

She knew it was early, but the darkness outside the window made time meaningless. There was only the cold, and the sound of wind pressing gently against the glass, like it was testing for a way in. She sat up slowly, pushing the heavy duvet aside. Her breath fogged in the still air. The radiator had gone cold sometime in the night.

3:17 a.m.

That knock, she wasn't sure if she'd heard it or dreamed it. A single sound, distant and dull. But it had planted something. A pressure at the base of her skull that hadn't left since.

She dressed in silence. Thermals, waterproofs, fleece. Everything layered until she felt sealed in. The mirror above the sink caught her eye as she zipped up her coat. She looked older. Or maybe just thinner. Her eyes were ringed and flat, like she hadn't slept for weeks.

She shouldered her pack and stepped into the hallway. The guesthouse creaked around her. Pipes groaning, wood settling. Old buildings always had their voices. This one just seemed to whisper. Outside, the wind cut through her layers in sharp little teeth. The stars were barely visible, faded by low clouds that hinted at snow. She clipped on her headlamp and walked down the empty street. Kinlochewe slept behind drawn curtains. Even the pub was dark. No voices, no lights, just the scuff of her boots and her own breath.

She reached the trailhead by 4:00 a.m.

The post stood crooked in the frost. She paused, placed her gloved hand on it, and exhaled slowly. It was stupid, but it felt like something should be said.

"I'm not here for you," she muttered to the dark. "I just want to know what happened."

The trail offered no answer.

But the stillness shifted.

Not wind. Not sound.

Just the feeling of something retreating. Or watching from farther away.

She turned once, looking back toward the dim line of the village road. It was gone. Not hidden. Just swallowed by mist and memory.

She faced forward again. Touched the post once more.

It felt warmer than it should have.

Or maybe her hand had just gone numb.

The first hour was all ascent.

Her legs burned with the climb, but she welcomed the pain. It kept her focused. Kept the rest at bay.

Snow dusted the higher ridges, but the path was clear enough. At least for now. Her boots found grip on rock and mud, though sometimes she slipped slightly and had to steady herself. A mist hung low across the glen, softening the landscape into suggestion.

The hills loomed like sleeping giants, and the trees thinned into skeletal lines before giving way to bare, heather-covered slopes.

As the sun finally began to rise behind thick cloud, the world remained grey. There was no golden light here. Just pale diffusion and shadow.

She stopped for water near a boulder shaped like a hunched figure. Pulled out a protein bar. Ate half. The taste turned to paste in her mouth, but she forced it down.

Far ahead, she saw the first cairn.

It stood beside the path, weathered and simple. A pile of stones stacked by hand. She remembered it from the last map Sorcha had drawn, just before her trip. It had been a marker, not of the trail, but of a choice. Sorcha had written in the margin:

"Left feels wrong. I'll go right."

Mara looked to the fork.

The right-hand path bent downhill, skirting the side of the valley before curving back toward Shena Vall. The left climbed higher. Not steeply, but steadily, disappearing behind a ridge that blocked the view. She didn't hesitate. She followed her sister's path. The trail narrowed. The mist thickened. And that's when she saw the boot prints.

Faint, fading. But there.

Mara froze.

She knew they weren't hers. The spacing was wrong, too wide. Heavier. And not recent, no detail left, no sharp edge, just the shadow of a print in half-melted snow.

One set. Headed the same direction.

Then they stopped.

She looked around, heart thumping. No sign of anyone. No echo of footsteps. Just her own breathing, too loud in her ears.

She moved on quickly after that, trying not to look over her shoulder.

She crested a small rise and found herself facing a lone tree. Gnarled and leafless, crooked against the white. It hadn't been on her map. It shouldn't have been here. Nothing should have grown at this altitude.

She walked past it slowly, unwilling to touch it, though it tugged at her eyes.

The bark was dark with moisture, but in one place it had been stripped, smoothed almost. As she passed, her breath caught.

There were markings.

Shallow lines, like someone had scratched symbols into the trunk with a blade or nail. A triangle. A spiral. And below them, a word etched in uneven strokes: "Wait."

Mara turned sharply.

The wind had stilled again.

And from somewhere ahead. No, behind. She heard her name.

"Mara."

Not loud. Not shouted. Just spoken.

She spun a full circle. Nothing. Just the hills and the tree and the high hush of snow settling.

She moved on faster after that. Not quite running. But close. She crested a low rise and paused. A tree stood there. A rowan gnarled and stunted, alone where nothing else grew. She was certain it hadn't been on the map. Certain it hadn't been there five minutes ago. As she passed, the wind stilled. The bark had been stripped in places, rubbed smooth like an old path stone. Symbols were carved there. Circles within circles, and that same inverted triangle.

Below them, one word: "WAIT."

Then: A voice. Whispering, from behind her ear. "Mara..." She turned fast. Too fast. Nearly lost her footing. No one. She didn't stop again. Not until the crooked tree was gone. Not until the whisper left her ears. Even then, something followed. A hush that wasn't silence but memory, trying to settle inside her bones.

By midday, the weather turned.

The wind shifted without warning, no build-up, no slow change. Suddenly colder. Meaner. The clouds sank lower until she felt like she was walking through breath. Visibility dropped to twenty feet. The path blurred. The trees, where they still stood, looked like charred bones. Her compass worked, but the needle wavered slightly. Not drifting, just jittering, like something magnetic was near. Mara stopped at a rock shelf to check her map, hands shaking more than they should've been. Not from cold. From something else.

She closed her eyes and tried to slow her pulse.

That's when she heard it.

A voice.

Faint.

Not words. Just a sound. High, drawn out, like someone humming in the fog.

She turned her headlamp back on, though it was daylight. It made no difference.

"Hello?" she called, her voice cracking in the wind.

Nothing.

She waited.

Then came the same sound again, this time behind her.

She didn't wait any longer.

She climbed. She knew she was close.

The air had changed. Subtly, but it was there. Thinner. Stiller. The wind still gusted now and then, but the rhythm was off. As if something larger was holding its breath, waiting to exhale.

Mara crested the ridge and paused to catch it herself.

Below, the valley spread wide and silent. The ground flattened out, cut by a black ribbon of river, flanked by patches of stubborn, frost-bitten grass. And there. Tucked into the curve of land, crouched low against the slope. Was the bothy.

It looked smaller than she remembered.

Not that she'd been there. But she'd seen photos. In the reports. On hillwalking blogs. The old stone hut had always seemed solid, reliable. Basic shelter for rough nights.

Now, it looked like a wound in the hillside.

The roof sagged slightly. The chimney leaned. The door hung half open like a cracked mouth.

Mara stayed still, watching it.

Nothing moved.

She adjusted her pack and began the final descent. Her boots slid more than once. The trail iced in patches. She caught herself. No injuries. Not yet.

Her breath came fast. She blamed the altitude. But her chest was tight in a way that wasn't just exertion.

Each step felt quieter. As if the snow muffled more than sound. As if it muted the world around her.

She passed a row of stones near the trail, man-made, flat slabs sunk upright into the earth. Too orderly to be natural. Not a fence. Not quite a grave. Just... placed.

Mara slowed down, eyeing them.

There were five.

She didn't stop.

The bothy's door creaked when she touched it. Not from rust. It was wood. But from age. The kind of slow, warped movement that sounded like complaint.

Inside: dimness. Cold.

And silence so thick it pressed against her skin.

The air felt wrong. Still, yes, but more than that. Stale, like the breath had been sucked out of the room and replaced with memory.

She stepped in, letting the door fall shut behind her.

Her boots thudded on stone. The floor was dry, mostly. Someone had left a plastic chair near the wall. A long-dead fire lay in the hearth, just black dust, and a few half-burned bones of wood.

There was no obvious damage. No blood. No sign of struggle.

But the room *felt* occupied. Like she'd just missed someone.

She dropped her pack near the corner and crouched, running her hand across the cold stone of the hearth. No warmth. Not even residual. The chill here was deep. Structural.

She took a slow turn around the room.

Her light passed over carvings in the wood, old names etched into the beams, messages from previous hikers. Most were harmless. Dates. "Stormed in 2018." "Cold but made it." Someone had drawn a crude deer.

One caught her eye.

Scratched, not carved. Jagged, like it had been done in a hurry.

DON'T FOLLOW THE SOUND

She stepped back from it instinctively.

There was more, below it, a second line, so faint she had to crouch to read it.

IT'S NOT A PERSON

She stared at the words for a long time.

Then stood, brushed snow from her shoulders, and set up her gear without speaking.

She lit the stove, half-hoping the hiss would drown out the silence. Heat crawled into the air reluctantly.

The light outside was already fading. She checked the journal. Her sister's. While the kettle boiled.

The last entry was dated a year ago to the day. Sorcha had written about reaching Shena Vall. Her notes were clear, upbeat. The bothy was "charming in a ruinous way." She was tired but happy.

The entry ended like this:

"I heard someone outside earlier, boots, I think. Thought I was alone up here. Might just be the wind…"

And that was it. No second page. No wrap-up.

Mara closed the journal.

The kettle whistled. She made tea from the melted snow filled her flask by inches. The taste was earthy, pine, maybe. But it was water. And it will have to do.

Later, as the last grey light bled from the sky, Mara stepped outside for a final look.

The world was still. The valley spread wide and empty. No birds. No wind.

She felt it again, that pressure behind the eyes. The sense of being watched not from a distance, but from within. Like the bothy itself was looking back at her.

She turned to go inside.

And then she saw it.

High on the ridge. Just for a second.

A figure.

Still. Long. Black against the snow.

Then it vanished. Not fled. Just ceased to be. Mara stared at the ridgeline. Her pulse thudded in her throat, but the real fear was quieter. It was the knowledge that something had looked back.

Every instinct screamed to deny it. Could've been a tree. Could've been a trick of light, but it hadn't been there before.

And the worst part wasn't that it vanished.

It was that she *felt* it watching her, even after it was gone.

The Bothy

Mara closed the door with more force than she meant to. The latch clunked into place, and for a moment, the sound echoed like a gunshot in the stone room. She turned and leaned against the door, her breath sharp in her chest.

She told herself it had been nothing.

A shadow. A tree. A trick of tired eyes.

But deep down. Below the logic, below the hardened, rational part of her that had made a career out of not believing in anything she couldn't measure. She knew better.

She peeled off her gloves slowly, flexing her numb fingers, and set them on the bench. Her breath hung in the air like fog, not moving. The bothy's silence was total. No creaks, no wind, no wildlife. Just her own presence, and something else that refused to be named.

She turned on her headlamp and let the beam move across the stone walls. The light hit the wood panel above the hearth. Names scratched into the surface over decades. Some were dated. Some were initials. Some were single words, almost like prayers: Alive, Lucky, Waited.

Then she saw it.

Her sister's name.

Sorcha Fraser

Clean, deliberate, carved in the steady hand of someone who knew exactly what they were doing. It was just above the old mantle, half-faded by time but unmistakable.

Mara felt her throat tighten.

She stepped closer and brushed her fingers lightly across the name. The wood was dry, rough beneath her glove. Her sister had been here. Had stood in this exact place. Had taken out a knife and carved her name like everyone else who passed through.

But this wasn't just a mark of passage. The bothy remembered her. Held her still. As if names weren't just left behind. Recorded. And then something happened.

Mara stepped back. The air felt heavier here. Not cold. Not exactly, but *dense*, like breathing underwater. She shivered and turned away.

That's when she noticed the others.

Lower down, near the floor. Symbols this time, not names. Spirals. Triangles. One long eye, unevenly scratched and smudged with black. A few lines that looked like runes, though she couldn't place them. All of them etched deeper than the rest. Fresh, even.

She crouched and ran the light along them. Someone had spent time here. Not passing time, not just carving initials like a bored hiker. These were intentional. Focused.

One symbol in particular drew her attention. It looked like a handprint, small, child-sized, but with elongated fingers. Not painted. Scratched.

The marks were dark at the edges, as if someone had dragged burnt charcoal through the grooves. But the wood around them felt freshly scored.

Too fresh.

As if something old had only just arrived.

She stood, too fast, her head brushing the low ceiling beam. The beam groaned. Not loudly, but it felt like a complaint.

She moved to her sleeping mat, unrolled it by the back wall, and lit the stove again. The flame flickered, fighting the cold. The bothy seemed to pull the heat away faster than it could generate it.

The kettle hissed softly as she poured water into a cup, then sat, watching steam rise and vanish into the dead air. The heat didn't seem to reach her hands. She drank anyway, just to have something warm in her mouth.

As the light faded outside, shadows gathered in the corners. They felt… thicker than shadows should. Less like the absence of light, more like something waiting for the chance to move.

Mara pulled out her journal and tried to write, just observations, facts, anything to ground herself, but the pen didn't feel right in her hand. Her fingers trembled too much.

Eventually, she set it down and lay back on her mat.

She told herself not to look at the wall again.

She looked anyway.

Sorcha's name was still there. Unchanged. Still carved, still steady.

But the other marks?

They looked deeper now.

And in the low, flickering light, she could've sworn that one of the spirals had *shifted*, slightly. Enough.

Mara didn't sleep. Not fully.

She drifted in and out, her body cocooned in the sleeping bag, her mind floating just above rest. Never quite tipping over the edge. Every time her thoughts began to blur, a sound would bring her back.

The bothy creaked in odd rhythms. Not the gentle stretch and sigh of old timber, but sharp, arrhythmic pops, like knuckles cracking in the walls.

Once, she thought she heard breathing that wasn't hers. But it stopped when she held her own breath to listen.

Sometime after midnight, the wind rose again. The air howled across the moor, low and angry, wrapping around the bothy like it was trying to find a way inside. Mara lay still, watching the door.

It was shut tight. She had made sure of it.

The temperature dropped further. Her breath fogged with each exhale, and frost began to creep along the inside of the glass bottle near her mat.

She pulled the sleeping bag tighter, turning onto her side to face the wall.

And that's when she heard it. Footsteps.

Outside.

Crunching slowly across the gravel and frozen earth. Deliberate. Measured. Not wandering, not hurried, *approaching.*

Mara froze. She strained to listen. The blood in her ears almost drowned the sound out, but it was there, getting closer.

Step.

Pause.

Step.

Pause. They stopped just outside the door.

Silence.

She sat up slowly, her breath catching in her throat. Every instinct screamed not to move, to stay small, still, unseen. But she couldn't stop herself. Her hand found the torch and clicked it on.

Nothing happened for several seconds.

Then. A knock.

Not the knuckle-on-wood rap of someone polite. This was dull. Heavy. Once. Then again.

Two knocks.

Then nothing.

Mara stared at the door. She waited for a voice. A greeting. Some sign of another human being.

Nothing came.

She moved to the window, but it was too dark to see beyond the frost-crusted pane. Just the vague outline of the slope, the distant glint of the river under moonlight.

Another knock. This time softer.

She gripped the torch tighter and stepped back.

"No," she whispered aloud, to no one. "No. You don't get to knock." The wind rose again, louder now, howling like it had something to say.

Then. Just as suddenly. Everything stopped. The silence returned. Complete. No more steps. No knocks. Just the hiss of her breath. She stayed like that for an hour, maybe more, seated on the floor with her back to the wall and her eyes fixed on the door. The torch died eventually, leaving her in the dull red glow of her emergency light. She didn't move.

Eventually, she forced herself to lie down again.

She didn't sleep. But she did close her eyes.

And somewhere near dawn, just as the black outside began to soften into grey, she heard something else.

A soft sound.

Inside.

Like a breath released in the dark. Just behind her ear.

The light came slow. Not a sunrise. A slow lifting of the dark. The sky outside turned from pitch to charcoal, then to the dull steel grey of a Highland morning. No warmth. No sun. Just the suggestion of time passing.

Mara sat up stiffly. Her neck ached from how she'd slept, hunched, angled toward the door, the emergency light still clenched in her hand like a weapon. She hadn't dreamed. Or maybe she had, but nothing lingered.

Only the breath.

That final whisper, just behind her ear. It hadn't been imagined. She knew what hallucinations felt like. She'd pushed herself to the edge more than once on solo expeditions. This wasn't that. It had had weight. Moisture. Intent.

She stood slowly, bones cracking in the cold, and crossed to the door. The latch was still down. The hinges unbroken. She touched the wood and felt the same rough texture beneath her palm. Her hand hesitated at the bolt. With one breath, she drew it back and pulled the door open.

Outside, the valley lay wide and whitewashed.

Snow had fallen again during the night. A thin layer, clean and untouched, powdering the earth in every direction. Mara stepped out slowly, boots crunching softly. She turned toward the front path. The spot where the knocks had come.

Nothing.

No prints. No disturbances. No sign that anyone, or anything that had come near the door. She looked left, then right. Scanned the area by the river. Checked the slope. Nothing. Not even her own prints from the night before.

The snowfall should've recorded it all.

But it was perfect.

Too perfect.

She stood there a long time, face turned to the wind, hands clenched into fists in her jacket pockets. The bothy behind her creaked once. Long and low, like a sigh.

She turned back toward it. Something about the building had shifted. Not structurally. Just... *presence*. It no longer felt like shelter. It felt like something watching her from the inside out.

She stepped back in.

Inside, everything was where she'd left it. Sleeping mat. Stove. Cup. Journal. But on the wall, above her sister's name. Was something new.

A fresh carving. Small. Sharp. A simple triangle, upside-down, with a line through the top. She hadn't seen it last night. She was certain. It hadn't been there.

She knelt and touched it lightly.

The wood flaked, the way it does when it's just been cut.

Fresh. Someone had done this *after* she arrived. Or something.

She stood again, this time slower. It was morning. She should be packing. Moving. Hiking out while the weather held. But she couldn't leave. Not yet. Something was wrong here. Something had taken Sorcha. Not a fall. Not exposure. Something else. And now it was trying to speak.

Mara flipped through Sorcha's journal in the headlamp's glow. Something scratched the edge of a page. An insert? She tugged gently. A fragment of a map, weather-creased and thin, slipped out. In one corner: a symbol.

Triangle. Broken at the top.

She looked again at the wall beside the bothy's window. There it was. Not carved. Branded. Beneath layers of soot and peeling whitewash, faint but there. She hadn't seen it before.

She traced it with a gloved finger. Her head ached.

The next journal line read:

"I woke up today and couldn't remember Mum's voice. I know I used to know it. I can hear everything else. The knock. The wind. But not her."

Mara blinked hard. She checked earlier entries. That line wasn't there yesterday. Was it?

She turned the page. The ink bled slightly as if the words had only just settled. Not written but remembered.

Her sister's last entry.

"Might just be the wind."

Maybe it had been, once. But not anymore.

Mara crossed to the fireplace, crouched, and stirred the old ashes. Among the charred remains of long-burnt logs, her fingers caught something strange. Smooth. Cold.

She pulled it free.

A button. Small. Metal. Etched with a thistle.

She froze.

It had belonged to Sorcha. She knew it. Her sister had sewn it onto her jacket herself. Mara had watched her do it on their last call before the trip, laughing at how proud she'd been to do something so "outdoorsy." She closed her fist around it, hard.

No more theories. No more excuses.

Something here remembered her sister.

Something here had *kept* part of her. And now it was speaking to Mara in its own slow, impossible way.

The hills keep what they take. This one. This valley, this black bothy, had taken something it wasn't finished with yet.

The Crossing

Mara left just after first light. The sky pressed low and grey against the hills, casting a light so dull it barely felt like morning. She packed methodically, not looking at the door, not glancing at the stone tucked away in her gear. She didn't want to feel watched, and the bothy made her feel that way now. Like it was more than shelter. Like it had a memory.

She stepped outside without saying goodbye.

The valley stretched out, the snow flattened and carved by wind into strange, looping patterns. It looked more like skin than terrain. She aimed for the gap in the ridgeline where she'd come in. A simple return. That's what she told herself.

Except the ridgeline had changed.

What should've been a clear descent had become an unfamiliar slope. The cairn she remembered. Gone. The outcrop where she had rested? Gone. The trail she'd memorised now curled in ways it hadn't before.

She pulled out her compass. The compass spun like a coin, refusing to land. Even the backup gyro pulsed aimlessly. As if direction itself had come loose. She closed it and marked a flat stone with a chalk X. Something to prove the world still held lines.

She headed east or at least what she believed was east.

For the first hour, she moved fast. The terrain shifted underfoot, but she kept moving. Over frost-stiff grass and a ridged bank of heather. A ridge crested. A narrow valley opened. She stopped. Caught her breath.

There it was. The stone. The same one.

The chalk X.

She checked the gouge at its corner. Same rock. Same direction. Same sky.

A pulse beat low in her temples. Not panic. Not yet. Just pressure. She turned again. West this time. Downhill. Through a clutch of bracken and across a dry streambed.

Half an hour. A crooked birch. A split boulder. A circle of standing stones, or maybe just weathered fenceposts. Then…

The X again.

Her mouth went dry. She crouched, ran her fingers across the chalk. Fresh. As if no time had passed. She added a triangle beneath it. Her own marker.

"East, then west," she said aloud. Her voice barely registered in the silence.

She chose north.

The valley shifted again.

The horizon darkened slightly, like a storm was building. But the clouds didn't move. The air didn't stir. Everything felt paused.

That's when she heard it.

A breath. Ragged. Wet. Like someone drowning slowly through cloth.

She turned.

Off the trail. If it could still be called a trail. Something dark slumped low in the snow. It hadn't been there before.

A deer.

Young. Small. Folded. The ribs exposed, the stomach peeled back with sharp, straight incisions. Not savaged. Not attacked. Opened.

No blood. No steam. The snow around it undisturbed.

Mara stepped closer. Slowly. Carefully. Its eyes were open. Wet. Wide.

She crouched but didn't touch it. Symbols marked its flank. Shallow carvings. Spirals. Triangles. A line through a circle. Ritualistic. Wrong.

She backed away.

That's when she saw the prints. Human. Barefoot. Long. Narrow. They circled the body once, then disappeared into a grove of scrubby, twisted trees.

She didn't follow.

She turned and walked. Fast. Any direction away from this.

But after ten minutes, her stomach turned. The chalk mark stared back at her like an open eye. The triangle was hers. But the circle wasn't. She crouched low. Ran a finger across the lines. Damp. Still soft.

"Someone's messing with me," she whispered, though she didn't believe it. Not fully.

No tracks.

No sound. Just this quiet, confident rewriting of the world around her. The kind of thing done by something that didn't need to rush.

Mara didn't hesitate. She ran.

Her breath came sharp and ragged. Her boots tore through snow and frozen heather. Every step landed wrong. The valley twisted beneath her, ground slanting where it had once been flat.

She passed the birch again. The split boulder. Then, a hollow stump she didn't remember noticing before. A curl of fabric peeked from its mouth. Red. Not bright. A dark, dried kind of red. Mara hesitated, stomach tightening.

She reached in slowly. The cloth came free with a brittle tug. It was part of a jacket cuff. Torn clean. She turned it over and froze.

A button was still attached.

A thistle. Etched in metal. The same kind Sorcha had sewn on herself. Mara had teased her for it on their last call: "Trying to cosplay a Highland warrior now?"

She dropped it. Then picked it up again. This wasn't confirmation. Not really. But it was something. Something real.

Physical. A thread between past and present, between sister and stone.

The wind rose like breath against the back of her neck. She turned, expecting trees. There were none.

She didn't stop to look.

Minutes passed. Or hours.

Eventually, the terrain blurred. Trees leaned in. Their trunks stretched upward too tall, too narrow. Some bent low, as if trying to hear her thoughts.

The snow grew patchy, then thick again. The cold numbed her thighs, her fingertips. Her mouth was dry with fear.

Then it changed again.

A clearing. Still. Silent. The snow smooth, untouched.

The same X waited in the centre. The triangle beneath it. And the circle below that.

She fell to her knees.

The wind didn't move. Nothing stirred. Her breath fogged slightly and then didn't. The air had stopped recording her presence.

She rose unsteadily to her feet, each movement slow and deliberate, as if her body were relearning how to obey her commands. Her legs trembled beneath her weight, the muscles tight with fear and exhaustion, but still she turned in place. One full, cautious circle, taking in the dim room that suddenly felt foreign, like it had shifted in her absence or simply revealed a truth it had been hiding all along.

Just as she began to steady herself, the sound broke through the silence.

A soft, mechanical click.

It came from her coat pocket.

The noise was small, almost inconsequential, but it cut through the air with unnatural sharpness, like the snap of a twig in a dead forest. She hadn't touched the recorder and yet something inside it had stirred. Her heart stuttered.

Then her voice emerged from the pocket, unmistakable but wrong in its cadence, flattened, detached, like something rehearsed or remembered poorly.

"Don't keep trying."

Every part of her stilled.

The air pressed in around her, thick with the weight of something unseen but utterly present, as if the bothy itself was listening, waiting to see what she would do next. Her hand hovered just above the fabric of her coat, unwilling to reach inside, unwilling to touch the source of the voice that had come from her lips yet did not belong to her memory.

The recorder powered off. Cold in her palm. She stared at it, then turned again.

The bothy stood ahead.

Closer now. Its shape wrong in the distance. Taller. Leaner. It didn't chase her. It didn't trap her. It just waited. Because that's what it did. It let you in when it wanted to remember you better.

But the same stone, the same roofline. The same door, slightly ajar.

She walked toward it because there was nowhere else left.

The air around her didn't resist. It let her come back.

When she stepped over the threshold, the room inside hadn't changed. But the warmth she'd tried to make linger was gone. The ashes in the hearth had scattered themselves.

Her footprints from the morning had been erased.

The bothy hadn't forgotten her.

The bothy was never shelter. It was shape. An outline grief could wear. A frame for memory's weight. Not to protect. To contain.

It had waited. Not as a place, but as a memory. A shape built from grief, from footsteps taken and voices lost. It didn't want blood. It wanted presence. It wanted to be remembered.

Mara stood at the threshold, stone in one hand.

"If you want to keep something," she said softly, "you should know it first."

She didn't run. She stepped into the bothy like walking into a story half-finished.

A voice. Not the Watcher's, broke through. Faint. Familiar. "Tell Mum I liked the oatcakes after all." Sorcha. Her voice. Laughing like it had before the hills called her name.

The sound unravelled her. It wasn't just a memory, it was her sister, passed back through the breath of the valley.

The door closed behind her. The bothy accepted her, stone and silence settling into place.

And the hills exhaled.

In the stillness, a new cairn rose, remembered.

Far above, on a ridge carved by no map, a cairn shifted. Beneath it, a second stone marked with a spiral. Now. Acknowledged.

In the space where stories become memory, and memory becomes landscape, Mara Fraser had not vanished.

She had become part of the watching.

.

The Talisman

Mara didn't want to go into the loft. But the recorder, had landed beside her again, turned slightly toward the loft this time. as if nudging.

She hadn't even thought about it. The low ceiling, the warped wooden ladder, the smell of old rot and dust. It hadn't looked like it led anywhere worth exploring.

But something pulled her there. Not curiosity. Not logic. Something closer to gravity. She found herself at the base of the ladder just after noon. Her boots had dried by the fire. The weather had held. Any reasonable person would've packed up and left. Mara knew that. Instead, she followed the pull. Like it wasn't her decision anymore.

She reached up and pressed her palm to the first rung. It was rough, splintered, and colder than she expected. The ladder creaked under her weight, joints shifting like old bones, but it held. She climbed slowly, each step a quiet argument between fear and resolve. The loft wasn't a true second level, a crawlspace tucked beneath the rafters. She had to crouch low, knees brushing old straw and splintered floorboards. The air was thick with dust, dry and stale. Her torchlight cut a narrow path through it.

At first, she saw nothing. Just empty corners, a rusted flask, a bird's nest long since abandoned. Near the back she saw the pouch. It was tucked behind a loose plank near the far corner. Small, dark brown leather knotted shut with waxed twine. She reached for it without thinking, like her hand had already made the decision. The leather felt soft, worn by time and fingers. She sat back on her heels and untied the cord.

Inside: a stone.

Not large. Palm-sized. Smooth, almost polished, but clearly hand shaped. Grey black, like basalt, etched with narrow lines that spiralled into a set of crude runes. The carvings were too shallow to be decorative. They looked more like instructions or a message for someone who knew how to read them. And on the inside flap of the pouch, barely legible, written in faded ink: *Sorcha Fraser*

Mara's throat closed. The name didn't bring comfort. It brought confirmation.

Sorcha had held this. Maybe even used it.

That changed everything. She hadn't just vanished. She'd been pulled in, into whatever the stone was part of. Mara's heart seized. She read it again. And again.

Her sister had put this here. She turned the stone in her hand, feeling its unnatural warmth, as if it had been held recently, as if it had *remembered* being held. Something in the carvings caught the light, a faint shimmer that shouldn't have been there.

Then something *moved* in the dark. Mara spun, hitting her head on the low beam. The torch fell. Darkness swallowed everything. Her own breathing now loud in her ears, the sound bouncing back at her too quickly, the air around her had shifted.

She groped for the torch, fingers shaking, finally finding it buried in the straw. She clicked it on. The loft was empty.

But it didn't *feel* empty.

She tucked the stone back into the pouch, slid it into her pocket, and backed down the ladder. The bothy below looked unchanged. Fire still burning low, journal still on the bench, door still latched, but the *feel* had shifted.

The silence was no longer neutral. It was watching her now. She sat down and laid the pouch gently on her lap. Her hand hovered over it for a long time. With trembling fingers, she opened the journal again.

No new entries.

No writing that wasn't hers.

Except, on the last page. Aa tiny smudge she hadn't noticed before. Just a faint mark in the corner. At first, she thought it was dirt. Then she turned the page toward the light. It wasn't dirt. It was a thumbprint. Pressed into the paper. Barely visible. But fresh.

One moment she was staring at the smudged page, the pouch still in her lap. The next, silence. Stillness. Thick as fog.

The bothy around her was unchanged. The fire was lit but gave off no heat. The shadows pooled too deeply in the corners. The light didn't touch them. And the door was open.

Not wide, just ajar, enough to show the edge of the night outside. A line of pure black. Heavier than shadow. Like it was *looking in.* Then she saw her.

Sorcha.

Standing in the doorway.

Still. Pale. Her rain jacket soaked and clinging to her body, hair flat with moisture, skin slightly greyed as if the blood had forgotten how to circulate. She didn't move.

Her mouth did.

Open. Close. Slow. Careful. She was saying something.

Mara tried to speak, to step forward, but her body didn't respond. She couldn't move, couldn't even lift her hand. Only watch. Sorcha's lips formed words, silently.

Then again.

Again.

Desperate.

Her eyes were wide, pleading. Then. S*nap*. Her head jerked to the side like she'd heard something. Not Mara. Something behind her.

Sorcha's mouth stopped moving.

Her eyes filled with panic.

She raised one arm. Slowly, and pointed *into* the bothy. Not at Mara. Past her. Over her shoulder.

Mara turned, but there was only the wall. The carvings. The stone hearth. She turned back.

Sorcha was gone.

The door was closed.

And she was alone. Her body woke with a jolt, drenched in sweat, heartbeat pounding against the inside of her throat.

The bothy was dark.

The fire was out. The coals cold. She hadn't let it die.

The pouch was on the ground beside her. The stone was out. Not in her hand, not in the pouch, but placed on her sleeping bag. Facing her.

Its carved surface gleamed faintly in the dark, as if catching light from a source that didn't exist. Mara grabbed it and shoved it back into the pouch, burying it deep in her pack. Then she listened. The wind still howled outside. Louder now, battering the walls. Inside the bothy...

Silence.

Utter, wrong silence.

No floor creaks. No shifting beams. No crackle from the coals. Even her own breath felt *muffled*.

Like the air had thickened.

Like the inside of the bothy wasn't part of the world anymore.

She stood, slowly, knees stiff, legs shaking, and crossed to the door.

Pressed her ear to it.

No sound.

Then, she noticed something.

Her breath, fogging slightly in the air.

Except… It wasn't fogging *toward* her. It was being *pulled*. Softly, subtly, away from her mouth. Toward the pouch. Like something drawing heat. Drawing life.

She grabbed her journal with one hand, the torch with the other, and whispered aloud:

"What *are* you?"

She didn't expect an answer.

But something shifted behind her. In the dark corner near the loft ladder.

Wood creaked. Like something repositioning itself. Mara turned, slowly, but saw only shadow.

She sat back down. Wrapped herself in the sleeping bag like armour. Kept the pouch beside her.

The dream hadn't been a dream. Or at least not only.

Sorcha had tried to speak. And Mara would find out what she'd said. Even if it meant staying here one more night.

Mara didn't sleep again.

She watched the grey light crawl through the cracks between stone and wood, unsure when night ended and day began. The storm had passed sometime after four. Not with a break, but a stop. Sudden. Like something outside had grown tired of pretending.

The bothy was silent.

Not peaceful. Just still.

Her breath came out normally now, but the cold had changed. It wasn't the kind that bit the skin. It sank. Deep, internal. A chill you couldn't rub out, like a hand gripping the back of your spine.

She packed slowly, trying to move as if it were any other morning. Boiled water. Ate. Took notes. But the rhythm was gone. Her thoughts kept circling back to the dream and the stone.

She pulled it out again, holding it under the light. The runes were clearer now. Or no. Not clearer. *Changed*.

She reached into her coat pocket to pull out the stone again. Except her fingers brushed fabric. Not leather. Paper. Folded, worn.

She unfolded it slowly. Her breath stopped.

A childhood drawing. Hers.

Crayon, faded. A house. A tree. Two stick figures with red hair.

She hadn't seen it in years. Thought it was lost with the rest of the old boxes. But here it was. In her coat. On this hill. And someone had drawn a third figure in the corner. Tall. Black. No face.

She stared at it for a long time, longer than she meant to. A part of her brain began quietly trying to explain it. Maybe she'd packed it without realising, maybe it had fallen into her bag during a visit home. But she knew that wasn't true.

She would've remembered this. The crease in the paper. The red smudge near the roof. And she definitely hadn't drawn the third figure.

The worst part wasn't that it was here. The worst part was that it *felt* familiar.

One of the markings had changed. What was once a closed loop now gaped open. She traced it slowly. The groove was deeper. Fresh. Like the stone had flinched in the night.

She hadn't imagined it. The stone had *shifted*. Mara set it down and stood, backing away slightly. The pouch it came from lay limp beside it, no longer hiding anything. She turned toward the door. Thought about leaving. But her boots wouldn't move.

Something in her, the same thing that pulled her up the ladder *wanted* her to stay. Not curiosity. Not even duty. Something more primal. Like whatever was inside the stone had a line in her now. She stepped outside for air. The sky was white. Snow still blanketed the ridges. The valley seemed untouched. The prints she left yesterday were gone. Replaced by wind-scoured smoothness.

She turned a slow circle. The river glittered. The slopes shimmered faintly in the morning light. Everything looked exactly how it should. Until she looked at the tree.

It was maybe fifty yards from the bothy. A lone rowan gnarled and hunched, like something retreating into itself. It hadn't been there yesterday. She was sure of it. The clearing had been empty.

But now? A single black string hung from one of its branches.

Mara squinted. Not string. Hair. Long. Dark. Still damp, like it hadn't dried since being cut. She stepped toward it, slowly. Each step heavy, like walking through water. Her torch beam jittered across the snow. As she approached, the light hit something else. Carved into the bark at eye level.

Not initials.

A symbol.

The same as the one on the stone, the now-open loop. Almost ritualistic. Sharp-edged. Fresh. She reached up toward the strand of hair. Hesitated. It fluttered in a breeze that hadn't touched her face. Then, behind her, from the bothy:

Three knocks.

Not loud. Not hurried. Just calm. Final.

She turned. No one was there.

But the door now hung wide open. The pouch lay on the threshold. And the stone had returned to it. She did not sleep.

And when dawn came, it was not light.

Mara stared at the stone. Its groove had shifted again. She could swear the loop was open now, like a mouth waiting to speak. "You wanted her more than me, didn't you?" she said aloud to the room. Not to the bothy, not to the stone, not even to Sorcha.

To whatever listened.

Her voice didn't echo. It landed.

For the first time, she felt the bothy pull back, as if startled.

Echoes

She flinched like she'd been struck.

The recorder was still. The red light off. Her voice. No. Not her *voice*. Hung in the air.

She tried to remember the last time she had really *heard* Sorcha's voice. Not the voicemail. Not the blog notes. Her voice, real, raw, and alive.

It felt like trying to hold smoke.

Click.

The recorder was still. Its red light dead. Her voice. No, not her voice, hung in the air like a presence more than a sound.

She tried to summon the memory of Sorcha's voice, the way it used to sound when they were children, laughing in the woods behind their house. But it blurred, always just out of reach.

Click.

The recorder hissed once and played four fractured messages.

First: laughter, warped, looping back on itself like a glitch in memory.

Then:

"How long have I been here?"

"You weren't supposed to find the stone."

"You never left."

And maybe that was the point. It didn't want to kill. It wanted to echo. To keep her voice in the room. A loop that made her real. Permanent. Mara backed against the wall, breath shallow. The stone in her coat pocket felt hot. Heavy. It pressed against her ribs like a second heartbeat.

She grabbed her journal with trembling hands. Flipped to a blank page.

Recorder activating on its own. Voice is mine but wrong. Messages seem predictive. Time? Echo? Possession?

She stopped mid-sentence.

Above, in her own handwriting, she found a single line she didn't remember writing.

"Don't listen to it after dark."

The ink was dry.

Her scalp crawled.

She flipped forward. Blank page. Then another. Then one with pressure marks. Something had been written and torn away. She shaded it with the edge of her pencil.

A faint line emerged: "It lives in the voice."

She snapped the book shut.

The voice was never the weapon. It was the doorway. Not screaming or summoning. Just speaking. Remembering aloud. The recorder clicked again.

"Run."

She didn't. But she dragged her sleeping bag to the far wall. Away from the hearth. From the floor. From the dark gap under the loft ladder. She curled into herself. Listened to the wind trying to remember how to blow.

Then. Just as her eyes began to close. A memory surfaced. Not hers. Not fully. The bothy blurred things. Sleep, memory, dream. There was no clear edge anymore. Time folded here. That's how it held you. A phrase flickering like static through old paper and smoke: "To read is to agree. To speak is to awaken." It wasn't something she'd heard before. Yet it felt lodged in her bones, like a warning someone had written into the margins of a forgotten book.

The recorder clicked again.

The recorder didn't stop. Every thirty minutes.

"She begged not to leave."

Mara wrote in her journal to steady herself. But her hand shook. The page she wrote on was blank, except halfway down, faint words had already begun to form. Not ink. Pressure. As if someone else had written them earlier.

"I'm not her. You want her, not me."

Her fingers trembled. She blinked, and when she looked again, the words were gone. Or had they moved lower on the page?

She stood too fast. The bothy tilted slightly around her, not visibly. But in sensation. Like a boat shifting underfoot.

"I'm not her," she whispered, this time aloud. "I'm not her."

The recorder clicked. Her voice played back immediately: "Then why do you sound like her?"

Mara backed toward the hearth. Her boots scraped the stone floor, louder than they should've been. Her breath came shallow and uneven. Something pressed against her temples, a rising pressure from within her skull.

She saw movement. Not in the room. In the journal. The pages ruffled without breeze. One turned itself. Then another. It stopped on a blank page. The pen, untouched, rolled slightly.

She stepped forward. The pen moved again. A single line scrawled itself across the top of the page:

"Let her speak."

Mara dropped the journal. Her voice cracked. "No."

The recorder clicked again, too fast, too eager. Her voice, distorted now:

"You've been speaking for her all along."

Mara screamed. At the recorder. At the journal. At the cold, heavy air.

The scream didn't echo. It stayed in the room. Wrapped around her. Held her throat like a second set of lungs.

She nearly gave in. Her knees buckled, hands gripping the stone edge of the hearth. The idea came slow but seductive: if she surrendered, maybe the pressure would stop. Maybe she'd hear Sorcha again, just once, clearly.

She leaned forward. The recorder waited. The pen rolled. The journal opened. One more page. One more message. One more memory. That's all. That's all it wanted.

"Sorcha," she whispered, no resistance left in her tone. "If you're here, just tell me what to do."

Silence.

A faint almost imagined. The knock. Three short taps from inside the bothy wall. Followed by her own voice on the recorder, murmuring something too faint to catch. The loop beginning again.

But something shifted. The final knock echoed differently. Hollow. As if from far away. And beneath it, a second voice. Quiet, barely more than breath...

"Run."

Mara froze. It wasn't her voice. Wasn't the bothy.

It was Sorcha.

A different weight settled into her limbs. Not fear, not surrender, clarity. The journal fluttered shut. The pen rolled back into stillness.

"I'm still here," she whispered. "And I'm not done."

The bothy didn't resist her this time. The door to the back room, usually stuck tight with rot and old stone, stood open. Not wide, but just enough. Inside, it was colder. The air felt peeled back. The room had changed. No shelves, no tools, no frost-laced window. Just a wall. Clean and black like obsidian.

Mara stepped forward. Her reflection did the same. But it wasn't her. Not quite. The hair was different, tied in a bun the way Sorcha wore it. The posture was too rigid. The mouth twisted in a half-smile she didn't recognise.

"You stayed too long," the reflection said. Mara didn't answer. Her hand tightened around the journal she still held.

"She's gone," the reflection whispered. "And if you want to find her, you'll have to leave you behind." It stepped forward. Mara stood still.

"Burn it," the reflection said. "Burn the book. Burn your voice. And she'll speak again." The journal pulsed hot in her palm. Her skin prickled. But her other hand, still pocketed, closed around the stone.

"I don't need to hear her," Mara said, eyes burning. "I remember her." She threw the journal into the fire.

The mirror shattered. Fractured beams slicing outward. The room blinked out. The bothy groaned. The recorder clicked once more, and died.

When Mara opened her eyes, the door behind her had vanished. But ahead: stone steps she hadn't seen before, leading up.

A draft of clean air reached her face. Pine. Cold.

She climbed.

"The handprint is older than the bothy."

"Ask it what it wants."

The voices overlapped, hers, Sorcha's, something else. One sharp, one distant, one woven from wind through stone. She turned, expecting to see someone behind her. There was no one. But the air pressed in, thick and expectant.

The journal pulsed faintly, like breath beneath skin. Mara stepped toward the wall. Her palm hovered an inch above the old red print, half-worn but unmistakable.

She didn't touch it. Instead, she asked, voice trembling but steady, "What do you want?"

Nothing answered. The temperature dropped. A gust pulled open the door. Outside, the mist had cleared. Just a little. Enough to see the path again. Enough to see the shadow at its edge.

She didn't know if it was Sorcha.

She moved anyway.

At some point, the light outside shifted again. A paler grey. Day, maybe. Or the simulation of it.

She pressed record herself. Just to reclaim the machine. "This is Mara Fraser," she said slowly. Her voice cracked. "Still at Shena Vall. Fourth night. I think. Though I swear I only remember two. Time's... loose in here..."

"Something is using the recorder. Playing my voice. Messages I haven't spoken. Time is... bent. Or listening. Maybe both. It's like the recorder isn't mine anymore."

She stopped the recording.

Set it down. In the corner of the recorder's base, something was etched. A line intersecting a triangle. Tiny, barely visible. She blinked, and it was gone.

The recorder clicked again without hesitation, as though it had been waiting. Almost eager, to continue. A new playback began, the static hiss preceding the voice now familiar, now personal.

"This is how it starts."

The words came in her own voice. Utterly precise, without distortion, without delay. It was not a replay of anything she had just said, nor a memory she could place.

It was ahead of her.

Not an echo of the past, but an intrusion from the immediate future, spoken in the same rhythm she was about to use, drawn from the breath she hadn't quite taken yet.

The cadence was exact: the same pause between syllables, the same slight hitch in tone that happened only when she was bracing herself. It was like hearing her own thoughts voiced a beat before she formed them, the sound cued from some inner reel she hadn't consented to roll.

This time, she didn't recoil. She didn't throw the recorder across the room or crush it beneath her boot. Instead, she stood motionless, the device cradled in her palm like something fragile and sacred and entirely dangerous. Her eyes fixed on it with a mixture of horror and reluctant reverence.

Another click.

And then, beneath the mechanical whir, came a whisper. So faint and low she almost mistook it for breath fogging in her ear.

"You never left."

She sat that way until the firelight became a suggestion. Until her fingers went numb.

And when she finally looked down, the recorder was no longer on the bench.

It was beside her sleeping bag.

And the red light was on. She hadn't changed the batteries since day one. It should've died in this cold.

She stared at the recorder where it now sat. Just inches from her sleeping bag.

She hadn't moved it.

The bench where she'd left it stood empty, undisturbed.

Her heart thudded once, deep, and thick in her chest. Not panic yet. Just that heavy, pre-thunder pressure before fear cracks through.

The red light blinked. Recording.

Mara reached for it slowly, as if afraid it might bite.

The plastic felt cold again. Colder than it should be. Like something had drawn the heat from it.

She pressed stop. Then play.

Static.

Then, softly: "You're not alone."

The voice was hers. Flat. Slower than natural speech, like a voice underwater.

She spoke aloud to the room. To whatever might be listening. "What do you want?"

The recorder didn't answer. Just clicked. And clicked again.

She stood abruptly, too fast. Her legs prickled with pins and needles. She paced once. Tight circle, four steps, wall to wall. Her breath felt sharp in her lungs.

She thought of Sorcha. Her voice. Her last message. That voicemail she still hadn't deleted:

"Still alive. The bothy's further than I thought… don't tell Mum I'm out of reception…"

Still alive.

She wasn't. Mara sat again, shoulders curling forward like something was pressing down on her spine. She rubbed the heel of her hand over her eyes, hard.

"I shouldn't have come," she muttered.

But even as she said it, part of her knew that wasn't true. Staying away would've been easier. Cleaner. This wasn't compulsion. It was guilt, shapeless and loud.

The recorder clicked. Playback: "But you did." She lifted her head slowly. Its voice. Her voice. Sounded closer this time. Less distorted. More real.

She turned it off. Again.

It clicked again. Recording.

With her jaw locked tight and her breath shallow in her chest, Mara pressed the stop button with more force than necessary, as if her intensity alone could assert control over the thing in her hand. "Stop it," she said, her voice low but charged with fury, not loud enough to echo but sharp enough to cut through the thick, breathless stillness that filled the room.

The recorder made no response. No click. No hiss. Just silence, cool and waiting.

She lowered it carefully to the floor as though it might lash out, placing it down as one might lay a body in a grave, with precision, with reluctance, with dread.

But as soon as she took her hands away, it clicked again.

The sound. Casual, mechanical, inevitable, it was more violating than a scream.

In one quick, impulsive motion, she snatched it up and hurled it toward the far wall, the action as much an exorcism as it was an act of rage. The recorder struck the stone with a dull crack, bounced once, and landed near the hearth with a hollow, final clatter that seemed to echo far longer than it should have.

And then. Nothing. No more clicks. No whispers. No shifting air or haunted static. Only the sound of her own breathing, uneven and audible in the quiet, and the heavy tick of her pulse pounding behind her ears like a second heartbeat.

She waited. Then, with reluctant resolve, crossed the room, her steps slow and deliberate, as if the short distance held more danger than a mountain trail.

She knelt beside it, her fingers hovering briefly before she picked it up.

The recorder blinked once.

Playback began.

"She's still here."

The words were delivered in her own voice, but with none of her will behind them. Soft, eerie, and certain, like a truth too old to question.

Mara's body locked into stillness, her breath caught on its way out. She froze, not just from fear, but from the unmistakable sense that the message wasn't meant to frighten her.

It was meant to remind her.

The flame in her stove hissed suddenly louder. As if the air had shifted.

She didn't respond. Just turned the device over in her palm. The battery indicator was still full. That made no sense. She hadn't replaced them in months.

Click.

"Don't stay past tonight."

She moved to her bag and unzipped it roughly. Pulled out the notebook again. Scanned her own handwriting for anything out of place.

One line had appeared in the margin of a page she swore she hadn't touched:

"Your voice is the doorway."

A doorway. Not hers, then. *Through* her. As if by speaking, she was making space. Carving a line the thing could follow. Words as cracks. Echoes as entry. She dropped the pen. Stared down at the page.

Then, suddenly, she remembered.

That night. Years ago. Sorcha had shown her a shortwave radio she found in an antique shop in Ullapool. They'd sat on the porch at dusk, tuning through static. Laughing when they caught half a signal. An old military transmission or garbled weather alert.

At one point, it had played back a piece of their own conversation with a delay.

Sorcha had grinned, eyes wide. "It's like it's *listening* to us."

Mara had said, "No. It's just bouncing around atmosphere."

But Sorcha hadn't stopped smiling.

"What if the atmosphere remembers?"

She'd laughed at the time. It had sounded poetic. Dumb, but charming. Like Sorcha always was.

Now, it didn't feel poetic.

It felt like a warning she hadn't understood.

Mara snapped the notebook shut.

The recorder was beside her again.

She hadn't heard it move.

Click.

Playback: "You're speaking through her."

Sorcha thought the recorder was neutral. A witness. But what if it wasn't? What if it *echoed* to invite? Her skin prickled.

"Who is 'her'?" she whispered.

Nothing.

She looked toward the loft ladder. Dark. Still. Too still.

Her thoughts scattered and rebuilt themselves into a question she hadn't dared ask before.

"Is Sorcha dead?"

She didn't expect a response.

Click.

Playback: "Not here." A pause. "Not only."

She backed away from the recorder, hand clutched at her chest like it could hold her ribcage together.

Click.

"She begged not to go."

Mara dropped to the bench, elbows on her knees, head in her hands. "I know."

Another click.

"Then why did you let her?"

Silence. The worst kind.

Not accusation. Just fact.

The kind of fact that burrowed under your skin and stayed there.

She didn't cry. She'd done that already. Months ago. Screamed into pillows, cursed the weather, cursed herself. Then she'd gone quiet. Hardened. That was easier. This was worse than the mechanical voices, worse than the mimicry of her own speech or the warped distortions from before.

This was quiet.

This was tender. This was the voice guilt wears when it decides to whisper instead of scream.

It didn't want to shock her, it wanted to break her open gently, from the inside. She stood still for a long moment, then spoke to the darkened room, her words barely escaping her throat.

"I didn't think she'd actually go alone."

The recorder responded with a click so soft it almost blended with the creak of the bothy's frame.

Then playback: "But she did." Another click, following too closely.

"And you didn't stop her."

Each phrase fell like a stone into water, no splash, no echo, just the weight of it sinking. Mara didn't answer. She couldn't, she didn't lack the words, it was the silence that followed seemed to demand reverence, rather than argument.

The bothy shifted around her, exhaling softly. A chill draft slipped under the door, curling at her ankles like smoke.

The recorder went silent. The red light faded. The mechanism stopped spinning.

It had powered off.

Finally.

But just as she began to release the tension from her shoulders, she felt something else.

A slow warmth rising from inside her coat pocket, unexpected, unnatural. She reached in with cautious fingers and pulled out the small leather pouch, the one she hadn't opened since arriving, not properly, not with intention.

Inside, the stone no longer slept.

Its carved surface glowed with a faint, pulsing light, soft and steady, each pulse like a heartbeat beneath a layer of skin. The lines etched into it, once so shallow they barely registered, now flickered with energy, delicate and precise.

It wasn't a theatrical glow. Not ominous or dramatic. Just enough to be seen. Enough to be noticed. Mara crouched slowly and placed the stone on the floor, carefully, between herself and the recorder, as though creating a boundary neither could cross.

As soon as it touched the ground, the glow began to fade. In gradual waves, like breath calming after panic.

The recorder clicked once more. Just once. Playback: "The doorway's open now."

Then silence.

No more recordings. No more messages. She sat until dawn.

Not trusting the quiet.

Not trusting her thoughts.

When the light finally came, dull and grain-grey through the slats in the shutters, she stood. Her body ached. Her skin felt thinner somehow, like the cold had scraped something off of her.

She reached for the recorder one last time.

It didn't click.

Didn't blink.

It was just a machine again.

But when she turned it over, she saw something scratched faintly into the back panel. Not etched by her. Not part of the make.

Three words. Shallow. Almost missed them.

"Say it back."

Descent

Mara left at first light. She didn't say goodbye to the bothy. Didn't even glance back. The door remained open behind her, like a mouth waiting for something else to step inside. She tightened the straps on her pack, adjusted her hood, and set off toward the ridge.

She expected the trail to be covered. The storm had made that certain. But she didn't expect this.

Everything was gone.

The cairns, the boulder she'd used as a landmark, even the curve of the path she'd followed up. All wiped clean. A flat white sheet stretched out in every direction, gently rolling, featureless. No contrast. No depth. No memory of footsteps.

She took out her compass.

The needle spun.

It turned once. Wavered. Then began circling, slow, steady, useless.

She tapped it. Waited.

Nothing changed.

She switched it out for her backup, a basic Silva, old but reliable. Same result. The land had gone still again. But not like yesterday. This stillness wasn't quiet.

It was *intentional*.

Like the hills had held a breath just long enough to let her pass and now exhaled, erasing every trace behind her. Mara picked a direction and started walking. She tried to use the river's position to guide her, but even the water seemed farther than it should've been. Each time she looked back, the bothy hadn't moved and yet she never seemed to get farther from it. After an hour, she stopped. Looked around.

She was still in the valley.

But now, it felt narrower.

The hills leaned closer. The sky had dimmed, though the sun should have been rising. Her breath fogged heavier now. Time stuttered. She walked faster. Focused on the rhythm of her steps. Her boots crunched through the snow. Her breath rasped in her throat.

Then came the sound.

High-pitched. Thin.

A child crying.

She stopped dead.

It came from the tree line ahead. Soft, wet sobbing, the kind that comes between breaths, hopeless and hurting. Mara turned her torch that way.

Nothing.

"Hello?" she called, hating how brittle her voice sounded. The crying stopped. Silence returned, hard and final.

She waited. Nothing moved. She took a single step forward. And the crying started again, this time behind her.

She turned. The bothy was still visible in the distance. So was the tree. And hanging from it now. Swinging gently. Was the lock of hair.

Longer than before. Mara didn't remember turning around. One moment she was staring at the tree. The long hair. The crying. Now silent again. And the next, her boots were dragging her back through the snow.

Back to the bothy. Back to whatever *waited* inside it. It wasn't fear, exactly. It was exhaustion. The kind that comes after resisting something bigger than you for too long. The wind didn't push her. The cold didn't rush her. It just *wanted* her back.

The door stood open when she arrived, as if expecting her. The pouch still lay in the same spot on the threshold. The stone inside it perfectly cantered, like it had never been touched.

She stepped over it and re-entered the stillness. Inside, everything was where she had left it. And everything was wrong.

There were *footprints*. Mud tracked across the stone floor. Not hers. These were barefoot, long in the toe, narrow at the heel.

Human-ish. But not quite. They came from the corner near the hearth, looped once around her bedroll, then vanished by the ladder to the loft. She backed up slowly, eyes sweeping the corners.

No movement.

But the silence was thicker now. Closer. Like the walls were listening. She crouched, examined the prints. They were wet, recent. The mud wasn't just from outside. It had a dark colour to it. Not soil. Something older.

She stood, heart hammering. She wanted to leave again. To run. But the path was gone. The compass was broken. She pulled out the beacon, flipped the cover. Pressed. Nothing. No LED. No signal. It was like the valley had swallowed the sky. The bothy, at least, was shelter.

She sat. Waited.

When darkness came, it did so suddenly, like a curtain falling. She lit the stove again, hands shaking. The flame struggled to stay lit, flickering weakly in the chill. She didn't eat. She just watched the door. Listened. The crying didn't return.

But something did.

A creak from above, from the loft. A slow shifting sound, like a body turning on old boards. Then stillness. Then again. Mara didn't move. She didn't breathe. The sound stopped.

She stayed that way for an hour. Maybe more. Then, finally, she slipped into sleep. Her body gave in. When she woke, she was standing. The door was open. Her hand was on it. Cold wind bit at her fingers. The moon was high. The snow reflected it back like dull bone. Mara didn't remember getting up. Didn't remember crossing the room. Didn't remember dreaming. She backed away from the threshold slowly and closed the door.

Bolted it.

Then sat back down and stared at her boots. They were wet.

But not from snow.

From *mud*.

After waking at the door, Mara sat in the corner with her back to the wall and her knees pulled tight. The bothy seemed smaller now or she was growing. The wind outside had stopped again. Not faded. Stopped. As if the world had hit pause. Even her breath sounded too loud. Every shift of her coat, every rustle of fabric scraped against the silence like static.

She watched the floor where the muddy footprints had been.

They were gone.

The stone was clean. No smear, no shadow, no residue.

But the air smelled faintly of earth. Wet and deep. The kind of smell you got when a grave was too shallow.

She stared into the dark until the edges of her vision flickered. Thought she saw a shape shift near the loft. But when she blinked, it was gone.

Then came the voice.

Soft.

From just over her shoulder.

"Mara." She froze. The word hadn't been loud. Just present. Someone was crouched behind her. She turned.

Nothing.

"Mara."

"You shouldn't have come." It was *Sorcha's* voice.

Her exact cadence, her warmth. But... flat. Off-key. Like a recording played a fraction too slow.

Mara stood. Her knees almost buckled.

"Where are you?" she whispered.

The room remained still.

"You left me."

"No," Mara said, louder now. "I looked for you. I *never* stopped." The voice didn't answer. The silence came back, thick, and complete. She turned toward the corner where the pouch still sat. The stone lay beside it again, face-up, runes glowing faintly like embers beneath the surface. This time, she didn't touch it.

Instead, she crouched beside it and whispered, "What are you?"

The room stayed silent. Then the floorboard beneath the hearth creaked. Not loudly. Just enough. She turned her light that way. Nothing. Still. She stood, crossed the room, knelt beside the hearth. There, under a thin layer of ash and stone dust, was a crack in the floor.

She dug with her hands, ignoring the cold. Splinters caught her knuckles. The stone was sharp.

After a minute, she found it. The edge of something wrapped in waxed cloth.

She pulled it free.

A bundle, palm sized. Wrapped tight with twine, sealed with what looked like pitch. And carved into the pitch. The same symbol from the tree. The open loop. The rune that *changed*.

She turned the bundle in her hands.

The room seemed to tighten around her. The air pulled taut.

The pitch felt warmer now. Not to the touch, but underneath it. Like something inside the bundle was holding its own heat. Breathing, almost. She brought it closer to her ear.

Nothing.

For a second, she thought she felt it breathe.

Not the bundle itself. But the air between her hands and it. A gentle pull, as if something leaned forward from behind the veil of the object, eager.

"It's just adrenaline," she whispered aloud, trying to ground herself.

Her voice sounded strange in the space. Sharp, too clean. Like it didn't belong here.

She placed the bundle down, gently. Backed away.

That's when she noticed it: the mirror in the far corner. It had been cracked before, but now the crack ran clean through the centre.

And for a second. Only a second. Her reflection lagged behind.

She lifted her hand. The reflection stayed still, then followed half a beat late.

She shut her eyes. Opened them again.

Normal.

But the panic wasn't gone. It stayed in her chest like a second pulse. Something not hers, not Mara's, vibrating in the bones.

Then: a scratch. Faint. From *inside*. She dropped it.

The sound stopped.

For a moment, she couldn't breathe. The air inside the bothy wasn't just cold. It was wrong. Dense. She staggered back, staring at the place where the bundle had landed.

The pitch had cracked slightly. Not broken. Just enough to let something seep through. A smell. Like ash, and something metallic.

Mara backed into the far wall and slid down, knees to her chest. Her watch said it was 2:17 a.m. When she looked again, seconds later, it read 4:42.

She hadn't moved.

The bundle hadn't either.

But her breath was fogging in new directions. Curling sideways. Toward the loft.

Then the voice again.

"You can't take it back."

"It's *in* you now." Mara dropped the bundle.

It hit the floor with a dull *thump*. Heavier than it should've been. She backed away, breathing sharp, fast, too loud in the stillness.

"You left me," the voice repeated, quieter this time. "And now you've opened the door."

The wind died sometime after midnight.

Mara woke standing. One hand on the latch. The door closed. The sleeping bag pooled behind her like shed skin. Her breath rasped shallow in her throat, pulse pounding.

She didn't remember getting up.

She didn't remember dreaming.

Only the cold in her bones and the sense that something had almost opened the door. That she had nearly helped it.

She stepped back from the threshold and forced herself to breathe. Counted to ten. Then twenty. The air in the bothy was wrong again. Not just stale, but heavy, like someone had been moving inside while she slept.

She turned.

The floor behind her was wet.

Not puddles. Tracks.

Boot prints. Leading from the far wall to where she now stood. Wide. Deep. Too large to be hers. Mud from no soil she'd seen nearby. Black, gritty, as if pulled from some place deeper than earth. They ended inches from her mat. Then stopped.

She didn't scream.

She wanted to. But the silence pressed her throat shut.

Instead, she dropped to her knees and touched one of the prints. Still damp. Still fresh.

Something had come inside.

Or never left.

The Watcher

The next day, the sun rose without heat. Pale and uncaring.

Mara packed her gear but didn't leave. The bothy wouldn't let her go yet or maybe she wasn't ready to leave what might be the last place her sister had stood. The valley outside stretched white and clean, but she didn't trust it. Not anymore. By midmorning, the cold had changed again.

It no longer stung. It pressed. Like standing too close to a silent, angry man. Mara couldn't warm her hands, even with gloves. The fire refused to catch. The air inside the bothy hung heavy, sour with ash and something older. The faint scent of wet stone and charred meat. She stepped outside, if only to breathe something else. The snow had settled into a hard crust overnight. Ice veined the surface, glinting under a pale sky. Everything was still. Too still.

She turned toward the path.

And stopped.

A man stood at the edge of the ridge.

Thin, hunched slightly, dressed in a tattered waterproof that fluttered even though there was no wind. His face was half-obscured by a hood. His arms hung slack at his sides. His posture was odd. Like a puppet dropped mid-performance.

He was staring at her. Mara's hand went instinctively to her pocket, fingers brushing the pouch that held the stone.

She took a cautious step forward.

"Hello?" she called.

The man didn't move.

She tried again. "Do you need help?"

At that, he did move. Just his head, tilting slightly. The way a bird studies something it doesn't quite understand. Then he took one step toward her. And stopped.

His mouth opened.

His voice was dry, brittle. Not like vocal cords straining. Like old paper tearing.

"Give it back."

Mara froze. "What?"

"The stone." He raised one trembling hand. "It doesn't belong to you. Or her. The hill marked it."

She stepped back. "Who *are* you?"

The man twitched. Not startled, but like something cracked inside him. A hitch in reality.

He said, more quietly, "You *woke it*."

A blink. And he was gone. No sound. No step. Just absence.

The place where he had stood was empty.

Mara ran forward, scanning the ridge.

No footprints.

Just smooth snow.

As if he had never been there. But he had. She heard him. *Felt* him. She touched her pocket again. The pouch inside was warm.

Mara didn't go back inside right away.

She stood there for a long time, staring at the ridge where the man had been. The air held no echo. No imprint. Just windless silence and the weight of his words.

"You woke it."

The pouch in her pocket pulsed with unnatural warmth. Like a stone left too long in the sun. There *was* no sun. The sky was still the same unbroken grey, lightless and flat.

She turned and looked back at the bothy.

It waited, open-mouthed. Her footprints the only disturbance in the snow now, leading back toward it like veins.

She needed to move. Staying felt like agreeing to something unspoken.

So she left. But the path didn't agree. Fifteen minutes into her descent, she reached a fork she didn't remember. One trail curved down, the other up. She chose down. Walked. Marked the rock with a notch of chalk. Twenty minutes later, the chalk-marked stone was in front of her again.

Mara stood in silence. No panic yet. Not quite. She checked her compass. North was the wrong way. She'd been walking southeast.

She tried again. This time following the higher ridge. Five minutes. Ten. Another cairn. This one old, buried under lichen. She didn't recognise it. But when she stepped past it, she found something worse.

A second bothy.

Not identical. Smaller. Broken. But the same shape. Same feel.

Inside, just darkness and a single burned-out lantern.

Her hands shook as she stepped back outside.

Then the wind whispered. Not around her. Through her.

And in that wind:

"Don't look back."

Her heart thundered. She didn't remember pulling out the stone. But it was in her palm. Warm. Throbbing faintly.

She closed her fist around it.

And walked on.

She re-entered slowly, every nerve sharp.

Inside, the cold was worse. No longer just winter cold. It was something deeper. As if the bothy itself had stopped acknowledging heat. She tried the fire again. Knelt by the stove, struck the match. Flame bloomed briefly... then vanished. Again. And again. No catch. No ember. The stove remained dead.

The air was heavy. She wrapped herself in her coat and sat on her bedroll, watching the door.

By late afternoon, the light had already started to go.

It was just after dusk when the figure appeared.

It stood in the doorway. Still. Watching. Not blocking the entrance. Just waiting. Tall. Black. Not clothed, just darkness in the shape of a man. No features. No face. A silhouette that didn't belong to the light.

Mara didn't breathe. The doorway framed it perfectly. Not quite blocking the entrance. Just standing. Like a statue that had always been there. She stared, heart pounding so hard it hurt her ribs. It didn't come closer.

But it didn't leave.

The last light drained from the valley.

Still it stood.

Her breath fogged the air in front of her. The cold had grown impossibly deep. Her fingers burned from it. Her lips cracked. Still, she didn't move.

The fire wouldn't light. The torch flickered and dimmed.

Still it watched.

She blinked once, her eyes dry and aching. Still it stood.

Minutes passed. Hours. Then, without a sound, it was gone.

Not walked away. Just *wasn't* anymore.

The doorway stood empty. The night beyond was black.

But the cold stayed behind.

And when she looked at her hand, still gripping the stone through the pouch, she found her fingers had turned white at the tips. She sat against the stone wall, blanket pulled tight, trying to will her fingers back to warmth. They ached deep in the joints. Not from frostbite yet, but from something worse: *a cold that didn't come from weather.* The fire had refused to light. Even the gas stove gave up. The flame sputtered and choked as if the air inside the bothy couldn't support fire anymore.

The temperature kept dropping.

Breath misted white, then stopped misting at all.

No condensation. No moisture in the air. Just dry, sharp stillness. Like breathing inside a sealed crypt. She watched the doorway, torch dimmed to preserve battery. It threw a soft circle of light that barely touched the walls. The rest was black. Heavy black. And the stone pulsed.

Still warm.

Still impossible.

It sat in her pack, but she could feel it through the layers. A dull, steady heat radiating upward into her spine. It hadn't cooled since she'd found it. Not once. She didn't dare move it again.

The Watcher had come to the door. Next time, it wouldn't stop there.

By morning, the bothy had begun to rot. That was the only word she had for it. The walls were damp now. But not from condensation. The stone *wept*. Thin trails of moisture ran between the cracks, dark and foul-smelling, like something underground had started seeping upward.

Mara woke with a sore throat. The air tasted of copper. Mould traced the edges of the ceiling beam above her. There hadn't been mould the day before.

And the smell…

Old soil. Stale water. The scent of caves no one had walked in for centuries. She stood slowly, legs weak from the cold. Her knees cracked. Her breath burned.

The mirror near the door. Warped and ancient. Was fogged.

She hadn't noticed it fog over all week. Not once.

She stepped toward it, ready to wipe it clear.

Then she stopped.

There was something written on the glass.

Faint. From a finger.

IT KNOWS YOU NOW

The words quivered slightly in the weak light.

And underneath them, her own reflection looked pale and distant. She was already fading.

The Journal

Mara didn't plan to search the floorboards.

She was moving without deciding, pacing the bothy to stay warm, to stay awake. Her torchlight swept the walls again and again, skipping over the same markings, the same stone, the same carvings that now felt older than time. Then, by the hearth, she stepped wrong. A floorboard dipped slightly under her boot. Not much. But enough. Enough to feel off.

She knelt. Ran her fingers across the grain. Cold, cracked wood. Dry rot along the edge. She dug her nails in and pried it up, the board splitting with a soft groan.

Beneath it. Buried in dust and splinters. A bundle wrapped in oilcloth. Black with age. Brittle at the edges.

She pulled it free and unwrapped it with shaking hands.

A book.

No. A journal. The leather cover had gone soft with moisture, but the binding held. Its pages smelled of smoke and mould and something olde. The way dead things sometimes do when the ground decides to give them back.

She opened it.

The handwriting was old. Sharp and neat at first, then increasingly erratic. The paper flaked at the edges as Mara turned the pages. The ink was faded, the spelling archaic, but the handwriting was neat. Deliberate, the script of someone trying to be understood long after they were gone.

"June 1823. The lambs are wrong this year. Born silent. Mother won't go near the northern stone. That place's gone odd again, since Davie moved the cairn."

Another entry:

"I told him not to. The hill's got memory. We all know it. You don't touch the stones unless you're ready to give back double. He laughed. Now he don't sleep. Says the trees whisper in a tongue he knew as a child but never learned."

The entries got shorter after that.

"Davie's eyes are black now, not with bruising. Just... empty."

"He walked into the glen yesterday. Didn't take rope. Didn't come back."

One page, scrawled more violently:

"The marker's moved again. The triangle with the cut. It's always facing the house now. Ma says it's the Watcher. The old one, the tall one. The one who waits in the cracks between breath. She says it don't want blood, just memory. Just to be known."

She reread that line twice. If it faced the house, maybe it wasn't a symbol. Maybe it was a direction. A pointer. Not away, but toward something. Toward someone. Mara turned to the final page. No words. Just a childlike drawing in charcoal. A triangle, upside down, with a line through the top. Below it: five stick figures. Four were crossed out.

Her breath caught. The bothy had stood this long.

She closed her eyes. It wasn't about Sorcha. Not entirely. It was about what she'd carried. What Mara carried now. The last entry was short.

Just three words, scratched in a shaky, barely legible scrawl.

It stands inside.

And then. A smear. Not ink. Not mould.

Blood. Fresh. She let the book fall shut. The bothy creaked around her. She turned toward the wall and saw the mirror again. Fogged.

But this time, *no words.*

Just a second face behind her own.

Watching. She spun around. The mirror was empty. Only her reflection now. Pale, drawn, eyes wide. Her breath returned in fast, sharp bursts, clouding the glass before vanishing again. But the face she'd seen. The one behind hers, had been real. Not imagined. Not shadow. Not dream. She could still feel the pressure of its presence, like static clinging to her skin.

The face hadn't been hers. But it looked the way her voice might sound. Stretched thin with memory. Like something trying to become whole. She crossed the room and knelt beside the journal again, wiping her hand across the stiff cover. Her pulse thudded in her fingertips. The book radiated cold.

She opened it, flipping past the final bloody entry, scanning backwards. Looking for *why*. New entries had been added to the journal.

He came from the hill. Eyes like black fire. I knew then the cairn had not kept him, only distracted him. And now I carry the stone. I carry the mark.

More:

The door will not open. Even when it is unlatched. I see trees that are not on the map. Paths that lead me back. The valley folds like paper, always toward him.

Mara whispered aloud, "It's a trap."

The path, the weather, the walls. None of it accidental. It wasn't keeping her safe. It was keeping her in place. Until the mark was ready. Until the memory was full enough to echo. The bothy, the land. The weather that shifted, the trail that vanished, the ridge that folded back on itself. None of it was a coincidence. She hadn't stayed.

She'd been *kept*. She turned to the first few pages again, seeking origin. Something that broke the cycle.

There, a sketch. Crude but clear. A stone. Carved with symbols. The same ones. She touched it, her fingertip brushing the page as if contact might unlock something. Beneath it:

Buried it once. It came back. Burned it. It came back. I thought maybe it needed to be seen. That if I recorded it, if I named it, it would lose its teeth. But I think I was wrong. I think it liked that.

I threw it to the river. Still I dream of the hill.

And smaller:

It doesn't follow the object. The object calls it.

That was the shift. Not cursed. Not hunted. Chosen. The bond wasn't a chain. It was a mirror. Each gesture, each word, made it more certain. You didn't wield it. You answered it. Her stomach turned. The stone wasn't cursed because of the Watcher. The Watcher *served* the stone.

No. Was *summoned* by it. Drawn to it, bound to whoever held it, *fed* by that bond. A line of possession across time. The crofter. Sorcha. Now her. Mara closed her eyes. Sorcha hadn't failed.

She'd just been first.

The one who opened the story. Not knowing it wouldn't end with her.

"You weren't weak," Mara whispered. "You just didn't know how loud memory could get." She turned one more page.

This entry was different. Measured, lucid. Like the writer had accepted something.

I believe the Watcher was once something else. A guardian. Or a warning. Whatever it was, the cairns held it. Not to keep it safe. To keep it still. The stone was a lock. And I... I picked it.

Mara let the book drop again, the words crawling across her spine like frost. She stood and crossed to her pack. Reached inside.

The pouch was warm. Still. She didn't open it. Couldn't. Instead, she picked up the journal and held it to her chest.

"Someone needs to see this," she whispered. "Someone who wasn't *me*." But even as she said it, she knew the truth: She wasn't getting out. Not yet.

Not while the stone still listened. Not while the Watcher waited. And the bothy. Breathing quiet and deep. Felt like it agreed. Mara crouched by the hearth, placing the journal open across her knees. The candle's stub flickered, barely enough to fight the dark bleeding in from the corners of the bothy. She flipped back through the crofter's entries, fingers scanning the lines as if she could extract answers from the ink itself.

"The triangle with the cut," she whispered. "Facing the house."

Sorcha had drawn it once, lightly, beside a weather log. No context. She'd written: "Maybe it's protection?" But it wasn't. It pointed toward the bothy like an arrow. Not a warning. A summoning. Her breath hitched. The same symbol had been carved above the hearth. And in her sister's journal. Sorcha had sketched it without context in a margin, just once, like it had come to her without meaning. Now it felt deliberate.

She turned to her own notes, rough scribbles about the stone. The spirals, the runes. Not Norse, not Gaelic, but old. Pre-language, maybe. Meant to be felt, not read.

"It don't want blood, just memory," the crofter had written. She understood that now.

The stone wasn't cursed in the storybook sense. It didn't kill outright. It anchored. It marked.

And once marked, you weren't prey. You were witness. Carrier. Like a living archive the Watcher could read. Maybe that's all it needed. Memory kept warm in a body.

What if the Watcher wasn't hunting? What if it was remembering? Sorcha had taken the stone. Touched it, maybe carried it. And the land had… noticed. Marked her.

And now it had marked Mara too.

A gust howled across the chimney mouth, deep and hollow, like something exhaling through stone lungs. The flame jumped. Shadows sprawled long across the walls. The carvings above the mantle shifted slightly in the light, like veins beneath skin.

Mara shut the journal and stood, slow and deliberate.

"If you want memory," she said to the dark, voice steady now, "then you've got it. But I'm not letting you rewrite it."

Reckoning

Mara moved without thinking.

She tore open the pack, scattering her gear across the stone. Stove, food, the journal, her backup torch. All useless now. Only the pouch mattered. Still warm. Still breathing like it had lungs.

She hesitated for half a breath. Just one.

Not from fear. From memory. The weight of the journal still pressed against her ribs. Her sister's words, her own handwriting, her voice trying to make sense of something senseless.

"Someone needs to see this," she'd whispered hours ago. But who? No one would believe it.

And that was the horror, wasn't it? Not the stone. Not even the Watcher.

Somewhere in the back of her mind, Sorcha's notes echoed. The stone didn't follow rules. It followed *intention*. Wanting to destroy it might not unbind it. Might even feed it. And yet, Mara couldn't let it sit there, humming like it knew her name. She needed to try. Even knowing the rules had already shifted. She looked toward the door. It was closed. But it felt like something beyond it was still watching.

"You wanted memory," she whispered, louder this time. "Then remember this."

She grabbed it, yanking the stone free. It didn't resist. It never did. It only waited. But this time, the weight in her hand felt different. Not like an artifact. Not like a threat.

Like a lock that had already failed.

She stood, crossed to the hearth, and dropped it onto the grate like a curse.

Then found a rock. Heavy, jagged. The kind that remembered killing. And she brought it down.

Once.

The sound was dull. Like stone meeting bone. Not shattering.

Twice.

Still nothing. No cracks. No chips. It didn't even shift on the grate. Her hands shook.

The third time, she screamed. The rock caught the edge hard.

The stone lit from within. A red pulse, like breath held too long. Not heat. Not fire.

Something older. Something escaping.

Not a weapon. Not a beacon. A seal. Broken.

Mara dropped the rock and stumbled back, breathing hard. The glow faded slowly, like the stone was laughing at her. She lunged for her knife next. Pulled it from her boot, jammed the tip into one of the runes, trying to pry it apart, to score it, *do something*.

The blade bent.

The handle scorched her palm. She dropped it with a sharp cry.

Her skin hissed. She screamed. Once. And bit it down.

A spiral bloomed in her palm, burned in perfect silence. Not just a scar. A brand.

She stared at it, her breath shallow and bright with pain. The burn throbbed. Deep, cold, wrong. The same symbol from the stone, burned into her flesh. The room tilted. The stone still sat where she'd left it.

Untouched.

The door to the bothy creaked. She looked. It hadn't moved.

But the air had. Not wind. Not chill. Just pressure. Like something *stepped in*. Mara stumbled back from the hearth and dropped to her knees beside the pack. She pulled the journal to her chest again, hands shaking.

She flipped it open. To the last page. Not the bloody one. The one *before*. There, in thin pencil, barely legible:

I tried to bury it. It came back inside me.

Mara closed the book.

"No more," she said. And then she heard the voice again.

Not outside. Not behind her.

From inside her own chest.

"It's not the stone," the voice said. Soft. From inside her chest.

"It's the opening."

The words weren't sound. They were understanding, buried too deep to unhear.

She opened her mouth to scream. To vomit. She didn't know which. But what came out was water.

Black.

Cold.

And endless.

The water wouldn't stop. Mara clutched her throat, body convulsing as cold, slick blackness spilled from her lips. Not spit. Not vomit. It came in *waves*. Thick as oil, tasting of iron and rot.

Her hands scrambled against the stone floor, slipping in it.

Then her body stilled. The pain didn't fade. It was simply *gone*, like her nerves had turned off. So had the room.

There was no more bothy. Only *darkness*, vast and humming.

And from within it: the sound of breath.

Not hers.

Sorcha's.

Mara blinked.

She stood.

Not in her body. Not exactly. She wasn't *seeing*. Not with eyes.

She wasn't dreaming. She was remembering something that hadn't belonged to her. Until now. The air was thick with damp and dread. Smoke. Moss. Wet wool.

Sorcha sat where Mara had sat. Same floor. Same fear. Her headlamp flickered like a dying heartbeat. Packs leaned in a corner. Her breath was fast. Too fast. But she was whispering to herself, a rhythm to stay calm. Mara watched helplessly. No sound reached her ears. Not properly. Only the low thrum of the storm outside. But inside, she could feel it: dread thick enough to choke on.

Sorcha turned suddenly. Not toward the door, but toward the mirror. She moved closer.

Sorcha's lips parted as if pulled by some invisible thread, and she began to mouth a phrase. Silent, repeated, compulsive. The movement was rhythmic, as though she had said it countless times before, in this place or others, to herself or to someone who had long since stopped listening.

Mara leaned in closer, heart thudding, eyes locked on the flicker of movement just behind the glass of the recording.

There was no sound. No audio to accompany the desperate forming of syllables. Only the shape of the words as they played across Sorcha's mouth like a ghost of language.

Four syllables. Over and over.

It's behind me.

Though no sound escaped Sorcha's image, the message was deafening in Mara's mind.

Then came the knock. Soft. Singular. Measured. It came from the bothy door. Not from the recorder, not from memory. It was real. It happened now.

Sorcha's image froze. So did Mara.

Then the second knock arrived, as calm and unhurried as the first, as though whoever. Or whatever, stood outside was in no rush to be let in.

A third knock followed. Slower. Polite. The sound of something mimicking civility, like someone taught to knock by watching people through a keyhole.

Mara's breath caught. Her hands were motionless at her sides, every muscle tensed against stillness.

Then came a fourth knock.

This one was different. Sharper.

Not louder, but pointed. Like a question asked with no intention of waiting for the answer.

The latch lifted *on its own*. The wind didn't push the door open.

The door *invited* the night in. Beyond it: nothing. Just a wall of black. *Not* shadow. Not fog.

Something blacker. *Thicker.*

It *entered.*

Sorcha staggered back, mouth wide in silent scream, torchlight cutting only inches into the dark mass now crawling through the doorway. Not a shape. Not a person.

A *presence*. Tall, skeletal, endless. Its face was not a face. Its eyes didn't shine. They *drained* light from the room.

And its hand. A long, slow reach. *Touched Sorcha's chest.*

Not hard. Just *marked* her.

Mara screamed. In real time. In memory. In every layer of self she still had. She tried to pull herself from the vision, to break the tether. But the moment kept going.

Sorcha dropped to her knees.

It started with a cough. Then more. Water. Not from her throat. From somewhere deeper. Cold, black, thick as rot. It poured from her lips in slow waves, choking her, soaking the stone floor.

She reached for breath. Found only dark.

Slowly.

To face Mara.

Though Mara was only a witness. A ghost. Still, her sister *saw her*. And Sorcha *smiled*.

But her mouth was *wrong* now.

Too wide. Too sharp. Too full of something that had *never been human*.

"We opened it," she said. Not a voice. A chorus.

"Now it won't close."

Mara snapped back into herself like a wire under tension.

Drenched. Freezing. Alone. The water gone. But the mark still burned.

And at the door:

A sound.

Three knocks. Low. Deliberate. Like someone asking politely to end her world.

Mara didn't move.

She sat on the cold stone, the last shudders of the vision still wracking her limbs, her ears ringing with Sorcha's voice. That *smile*. That *thing* inside her sister's face. Outside, nothing stirred.

The fire was long dead. The stone sat untouched on the hearth, but the light in it now pulsed steadily, like a heartbeat.

She knew what it wanted. It had never been about worship. Or superstition. It was *ritual*. The stone was the key. The bothy was the gate. And she. She was just the next hinge.

Mara stood. The pain in her palm had deepened. The mark no longer just a burn. It pulsed, matching the stone's rhythm.

She walked toward the door.

Somewhere, the recorder clicked one last time. But it didn't play her voice. It waited.

No torch. No boots. No pack.

Just her breath. Her mark. Her fear. And something else now: *resolve*. The air outside wasn't cold. Not exactly.

It was *absent*.

No temperature. No scent. No sound.

The forest was still there, but wrong. Tall, bending slightly inward, as if listening. Watching. And the path? Gone. Erased.

Instead, stones. Wide, flat, wet with mist. Led away from the bothy like a trail of bones.

Mara followed.

Each step heavier than the last, as if the land pulled at her, trying to hold her here or pull her *through*.

Then the hill. Not high, but ancient. A squat rise covered in twisted grass and gorse. And at the summit: the cairn.

No longer collapsed. Rebuilt.

Perfect.

Someone. Or something. Had restored it. But the stones didn't look dry. They looked wet. With blood. With time. With *memory*.

Mara climbed. At the top, the Watcher waited.

It did not pretend now.

No disguise of mist or tree-shadow.

She stopped just short of the summit. Her breath rasped in shallow bursts, but it wasn't the climb. It was the moment. The kind of weight that feels like more than gravity.

In her coat pocket, the stone pulsed once. Heat sharp enough to sting. She didn't flinch. She looked down at her hand, at the faint scar burned into the skin.

"You took her," she said aloud.

The words didn't echo. They didn't need to.

"And you want me next."

She felt the truth in that. Not possession. Not death. Witness.

It didn't want to kill her.

It wanted to remember her.

She looked up. The thing at the cairn watched her. Not with eyes. With *intention*. A pulling weight, like her name being spoken without sound.

"You don't get to finish the story," she said.

It didn't want to end her. That wasn't the shape of the horror. It wanted her to carry the echo. To walk back into the world changed. A vessel for what should have been forgotten.

And stepped forward.

It stood twelve feet tall. Skeletal, robed in moving dark, its face an absence. Its arms hung too long. Its fingers ended in splintered stone. And its eyes… if they could be called that… pulled at the edges of thought. Mara stopped ten feet away.

The stone in her hand vibrated.

The Watcher reached.

It wanted *her* to give it.

To *offer*.

To complete the loop. Mara looked down at the stone. Felt its heat, its call. And then she looked behind her.

The path was gone.

The bothy. gone. Only black trees in all directions now.

No return. No retreat.

She stepped forward. Held out her hand. But not to give.

To drop.

She let the stone fall at the Watcher's feet. Nothing happened.

Until she whispered: "You can't have me."

Then everything moved. The sky cracked. Not with light or thunder, but with soundless pressure.

The ground shook. The cairn collapsed inward, like a throat swallowing.

The Watcher screamed. Not aloud, but *inside her head*. A pressure that split thought from bone. It reared, furious, blind. But not toward her.

Toward the stone. The talisman had been offered. But not in submission. In *defiance*.

And that act. Single refusal. Disrupted the cycle.

Mara turned and ran.

Down the hill. Into the dark.

Behind her, the cairn folded into the earth, the Watcher pulled with it. Roaring across time.

She woke at dawn. Curled beneath a pine tree. Her hand burned, the mark still there.

But the bothy?

Now a ruin. Just two walls left standing. No roof. No hearth. The door lay flat on the ground. And no sign of the stone.

Or of the Watcher.

Or of Sorcha.

Only silence.

And the slow, cold wind across the glen.

Offering

The frost clung to the tips of her fingers as Mara stood, stiff and aching under the weak Highland sun. She hadn't slept so much as blacked out. Her boots were still wet, the inside of her pack scattered across the pine needles.

The bothy was gone. Not burned or damaged, just... returned to age. Two stone walls, one leaning, the other crumbled. Like the rest had been peeled away or never existed at all. Maybe it was never a place, not really. Just a mask the land wore when it wanted to be seen.

And yet.

The burn on her hand still throbbed. The air still held the same electric stillness, like a breath being held by the land itself.

And in her pack, buried in a side pocket she swore she hadn't touched. The talisman.

Wrapped in cloth. Cold as ice. Still humming.

Mara didn't scream. Didn't curse. Just stood there, staring at the trees. Then she pulled out the journal. Her thumb skimmed over the brittle pages, stopping at the only location mentioned twice: a cairn to the south, older than the rest, behind a split boulder shaped like a crooked jaw. The crofter had tried to return the stone there. "To seal the line," he'd written.

Seal the line. End the pull. That was her only hope.

She tucked the talisman deeper into her coat, shouldered the pack, and stepped off what remained of the bothy's foundation. The land didn't welcome her, but it let her move. That was enough. The path was barely that. Deer trails and frost-shattered mud banks. Trees clawed low over her head. Somewhere nearby, water trickled under ice.

The Watcher didn't appear, not directly.

But it was near.

She could feel it now. Not like before, not as a looming shadow or a dream. This was proximity. Real. Physical. *Hunting*.

Every time she stopped, so did the world.

Every time she blinked, the trees looked subtly different.

Every hour, she heard something just behind her. A footstep that didn't match hers. A twig snapping. A breath not her own.

At one point, she stepped over a small ridge and saw footprints. Her own, circling back toward her. She didn't stop. She didn't speak. Just walked faster.

By late afternoon, the sky dimmed again.

She found the crooked boulder by accident, tucked against a hillside, lichen-covered and strange in shape, like two broken teeth jutting from the earth. Behind it, the cairn rose low and wide, not like the other one. This was older, built not to mark a death but to hide something.

She took the talisman out, hands trembling.

She didn't speak. She didn't offer words.

Just placed it. Slowly, firmly. Into the hollow space near the cairn's base. Then stood back. The wind stilled.

The cold seemed to lift, just a little.

And for the first time in days, she felt *alone*.

She exhaled. And sat on a stone, heart hammering, her eyes wet with exhausted relief.

That was it.

It was done. Until the world dropped into silence so deep it made her ears ring. And she saw the shadow stretch across the clearing.

It hadn't worked. Because it was never about peace. It was about witness. The shadow slid forward like oil down stone.

Mara didn't turn to run. She stood. Every cell in her body screamed for flight, but something else. Something deeper. Held her still.

It was not bravery.

It was *acceptance*.

The trees surrounding the clearing began to bow inward, as if forced by wind, but no wind blew. The sky turned pale grey, drained, not dimmed. And the stone cairn behind her, once old and still, began to *hum*.

She could feel it in her ribs.

The Watcher stepped into view.

No cloak. No tricks.

A shape too tall, too thin, its joints wrong, its head tilted at a sick angle. No face, but a smooth plane of shifting black, like wet rock reflecting things not present. It stopped six feet from her.

They stood like that for a moment. Mara breathing hard, the Watcher utterly still. Then, slowly, it raised one arm.

A long, stony finger pointed to her chest.

Mara shook her head.

"No," she whispered. "I returned it. It's done."

The figure didn't move. It didn't have to. The talisman wasn't the end. It was the beginning. A mark. A summons.

What mattered was the story. The *line* of it. A thread stitched through every person who carried that stone. Witnesses. Bearers.

The Watcher wasn't just a warden of land, cairn, or curse.

It was a thing fed by memory.

It didn't watch with hatred. It watched because it couldn't forget. Couldn't let go. It was memory. Not malice. And now she was inside the story too. And now Mara had walked every step. Seen every page. Carried the stone. Spoken the words.

It didn't want the talisman. It wanted her.

She turned and ran. Not out of hope. Out of instinct.

Through the narrow trail, down the side of the ridge. Leaping frozen gullies, snapping branches as she went. Her legs screamed. Her lungs burned. The Watcher didn't chase in the way people did.

It just appeared. Ahead of her, to the left, then to the right, always just beyond the next tree.

Not blocking. *Witnessing.*

It didn't need to kill her.

It just needed her to see it. Truly see it. And carry that horror forward.

That was the offering.

She broke into a clearing, stumbled over a root, and fell. Hard her forehead smacking stone. Everything went white.

Then *black*.

Then something between.

She opened her eyes slowly. Not in the forest. Not on the hill.

She was in the bothy again.

The room was still. Warm. Whole, like nothing had ever gone wrong. The fire flickering. Sorcha sat across from her, hair braided, smiling softly. Like she'd never left. Like the hills hadn't swallowed her whole.

"Hi," she said.

"You left me," Mara whispered.

"I didn't mean to." Sorcha's voice cracked. "I just wanted to see what it meant."

"And?"

"It meant me."

The air pulsed. The bothy shivered.

"I carried it," Sorcha said softly. "Too long. I thought I could document it. But it was documenting me."

Mara stepped forward. Her knees nearly buckled. "Why didn't you leave anything behind?"

Sorcha's voice cracked. "I did. It just hides what it doesn't want you to see."

She looked over Mara's shoulder. "You're still whole. Don't let it unmake you."

"Mara," Sorcha said, eyes pleading, "Don't let it remember you." Silence swallowed the room. Thick. Final.

Then Mara asked, "What is it?" Sorcha turned toward the door. The latch lifted. Slow and soundless.

"It heard me," she whispered. "It's what memory becomes when no one's watching."

"It *was* human. Once."

"Now it's just… story. Hunger and shadow. And us."

The voice lingered in her skull like smoke.

Mara couldn't tell if her eyes were open. The dark felt endless. But somewhere behind her ribs, something cracked—not bone, not pain. A release. She felt her body. Not fully. But the weight of it. Cold. Damp. Real.

And then another voice. Her own. Whispering through the black: *"Say it back."*

Then silence again.

Not empty.

Listening.

Mara woke. For real this time. Lying at the foot of the cairn. The sky above her was full of morning light.

No Watcher.

No shadow.

But deep in her palm, the burn glowed faintly.

Still there.

Still alive.

She got up. Shouldered her pack.

And began walking. Away from the cairn, toward the coast.

Mara walked for two days. No Watcher. No dreams. No stone.

Just sky, frost, and silence. She passed no one on the way out of the glen. No hikers. No animals. Only the landscape. Watching, holding its breath. It wasn't until she reached the gravel forestry road that her legs buckled. She collapsed by a rusted gate, blinking into the pale light, unsure if she was crying or just too dry to manage it.

A farmer found her three hours later. Old man in a Land Rover. Asked no questions. Just gave her water, wrapped her in a scratchy wool blanket, and drove. She didn't speak until they reached Kinlochewe.

Even then, only one word.

"Phone."

The ride back blurred. She remembered the heater blasting but still feeling cold. Remembered the man's hands. Rough, careful.

As he tucked the blanket tighter around her shoulders. Outside the window, the hills receded like waves pulling back from shore.

When they passed the turnoff to the bothy trail, she didn't look.

The man didn't ask what she'd seen.

At one point, he glanced at her in the rearview mirror. "You lose someone?"

Mara didn't answer.

But the look on her face told him enough.

He didn't speak again.

The police were kind.

She told them she'd been looking for her sister, gotten lost in the snow, stayed in the bothy.

They didn't question much. Her face said enough.

An officer, young, nervous, told her Sorcha's case had gone cold last winter. Weather made recovery impossible. No body ever found. Mara nodded, hands flat on the table.

She knew why.

They offered her a room at the station to rest. She declined.

Instead, she checked into the inn by the loch, same place her sister had stayed that first night a year ago.

The room smelled like damp pine and old bedsheets.

Mara stood by the window until dark.

She didn't eat.

She didn't sleep.

She just *watched* the treeline across the water. The next morning, she woke to birdsong.

It felt wrong. Too normal.

She opened her palm. The burn had faded. Mostly, but the shape of the runes remained, ghosted there like a scar only she could see. She tried to draw them once, on hotel notepaper. But when she looked back down, the lines were gone. The ink had bled. The paper torn.

She never tried again.

The days that followed didn't feel real.

She stayed in the hotel longer than she meant to. Slept with the light on. Refused housekeeping. Ate quietly in the corner of the breakfast room, listening to other guests talk about weather and hiking gear and ferry timetables.

At night, she kept the recorder on the nightstand. Just in case.

It never clicked again.

But once, just before sleep, she thought she heard Sorcha's voice from the room next door. Laughing. She pressed her hand to the wall. Nothing.

A week passed.

Mara returned home to Glasgow. Her flat looked smaller than she remembered. Louder. She unplugged the clock. Took down the mirror in the hallway. The sound of the city at night helped. Somewhat. But some nights. Especially when it rained. She'd wake at 2:13 a.m.

And the *door* would be open.

Just an inch.

She always closed it.

She never locked it.

She didn't dare.

Some nights, she stayed on the sofa, watching the hallway until sunrise. She stopped using her bedroom. The recorder sat on her kitchen table like a centrepiece. She couldn't bring herself to throw it away. A few times, she pressed play.

Just static.

But that was almost worse.

Something about the silence felt *expectant*, like it was waiting for her to speak first.

A month later, she was in a second-hand bookshop in Finnieston when she saw it. A thin leather-bound journal. Old. Unlabelled. But she *knew* the cover.

Same kind of leather. Same stitching. Same smell. She opened it slowly. Inside: a map. Of the Highlands. A route drawn in red ink.

To another cairn. A different hill. But the runes were the same.

Beneath the map, one line: *"The watcher waits. The line continues."*

Mara closed the book and bought it.

She didn't ask who brought it in. She didn't want to know.

On the walk home, the sky was overcast. At the next crosswalk, the light flickered.

She didn't wait.

She kept walking.

The Hill

It was late March when they went looking.

The snow had receded to stubborn veins along the ridgelines, the rivers were running fat with meltwater, and the air in Glen Shiel had the tentative warmth of a season trying to turn.

Two walkers. A retired couple from Inverness. Had taken a wrong trail somewhere past the forestry gates. They meant to loop back toward the Munros but instead followed an old deer path that led them too high, too far east. The woman's knee had started acting up. They decided to cut across the glen, find a place to rest before dusk.

They hadn't expected to find the bothy.

At first, they didn't even recognise it as such. It looked derelict. Stones shifted, door hanging crooked, chimney slumped.

But the door creaked open. There was still shelter. That's all a bothy needs to be.

The man stepped inside, muttering something about poor maintenance.

Then he saw the pack.

It was propped neatly in a corner. Zipped, rain cover still in place, like someone had left it there yesterday. Inside: spare socks, a cracked phone, a notebook, half a chocolate bar, and a receipt from a Spar in Kinlochewe dated six weeks ago.

No sleeping bag. No coat. No sign of food preparation. No boots. The woman glanced around, uneasy. "Maybe she meant to come back."

He shook his head. "Not in March. Not without gear."

She stepped toward the far wall, her eyes adjusting to the dim. "Look at this."

Near the hearth, in the low wood panelling beside the stonework, someone had carved a message. Not new, not old.

Just deep enough to last.

DON'T STAY PAST DARK IT WATCHES

The man stared at it for a long moment.

Then zipped the pack and set it by the door.

They left before the sun dipped behind the ridge.

Neither of them spoke again until they hit the road.

They didn't speak during the hike down. The path looked different on the return. Too narrow, then too wide, like the land couldn't decide how to hold them. The older man glanced back only once. The bothy was already gone.

Not hidden.

Just gone.

That night, in the pub, the younger man tried to ask what he'd seen. The other just said, "If it let us go, we don't ask why."

A week later, the mountain rescue team came.

Two officers, both used to call like this. Old cases resurfacing, tourists getting lost, packs found with no owners.

They logged the discovery. Packed up the bag. Made notes.

Searched the area within a two-mile radius.

Nothing.

No footprints, no campsite, no clothing. No bones.

The bothy was logged as "abandoned and unsafe."

They nailed a warning to the door.

Then left.

The bothy stood quiet after they went.

That's when it breathed again. Not a refuge. Not anymore. It doesn't shelter. It collects.

For a while, the wind didn't return.

The clouds hung motionless over the ridge, as if the sky itself were waiting.

Inside, dust settled in the shape of a handprint near the hearth.

Just one.

The recorder sat where it always had. No blinking light.

But if you stood close enough. If you waited long enough. You could almost hear it click.

Three days later, another hiker found it.

He wasn't from the area.

Mid-thirties, solo backpacker, making his way north toward Torridon. He saw the bothy just before nightfall. A square of shadow against the heather, distant but sheltering. When he pushed the door open, it moaned loud enough to echo.

Inside, the air was sharp with cold.

Dust hung in the light from his headtorch.

He set down his bag and gave the place a once-over. Didn't notice the warning carved in the wall just yet. Didn't feel the temperature drop behind him. Didn't see the *shadow shift in the corner*. Too slow to be wind, too tall to be trick of light.

He exhaled. Rolled his shoulders. Sat on the edge of the stone hearth and somewhere behind him, a board creaked underweight not his own.

The wind picked up as the hiker unpacked.

It had a strange sound to it. Less of a howl, more of a *sigh*. Long and low, like breath over glass. He zipped his jacket higher and muttered a curse about the cold.

His name was Nathan. He'd started in Glenfinnan four days ago, moving light and fast, sleeping rough. The bothy had been a welcome surprise. Real shelter. Stone walls. A roof. Even a cold fireplace and an old chair with three legs.

He sat and boiled water over his stove. Ate noodles. Journaled. The usual routine.

And still. That feeling.

Not fear. Just that *someone was watching*.

He checked outside. Nothing but dusk and drifting mist.

Inside again, he noticed the carvings. Dozens, under years of soot and grime.

Initials. Dates. Scratched warnings.

He crouched closer.

One stood out. Deeper than the others. Angled strangely.

DON'T STAY PAST DARK IT WATCHES

He gave a short laugh. "Alright then," he muttered to himself, snapping a picture with his phone. "Classic ghost story stuff."

He wasn't afraid. He was tired. Wind-chapped. Half-ready to fall asleep sitting up.

So he laid out his mat, crawled into his bag, and left the headtorch on.

Just for comfort.

Just for the dark.

The stillness inside the bothy felt thick, like a held breath.

Nathan lay still for a long time, not quite asleep, not fully awake. The kind of half-space where thoughts slide in sideways.

He meant to turn the recorder off but forgot.

It sat just beside his pack. Quiet.

Once, he thought he heard something. A scratch. Maybe the stove settling. Maybe not.

But he didn't check.

At 2:13 a.m., the torch flickered.

Once.

Twice.

Then went out.

Nathan opened his eyes to perfect black.

The kind of dark that presses against your face, which makes your ears ring with the absence of sound.

He sat up slowly.

The wind outside had stopped.

The world was still.

Too still.

His breath felt loud. Too loud. He clamped his mouth shut.

In the corner of the room. The darkest part. Something shifted.

A creak. The stretch of timber underweight. Nathan turned toward it, heart kicking hard against his ribs. He saw *nothing*. But he *felt it*. Like heat. Or pressure. Or *presence*. Slowly, he reached for the headtorch.

It clicked.

Nothing.

Clicked again.

The beam burst to life. And for a split second, he thought he saw legs. Long. Jointed wrong. Standing still. But when he aimed the torch fully, the corner was empty. His heart wouldn't slow. He didn't sleep the rest of the night. At first light, he packed in silence.

Left without breakfast.

Didn't look back.

He made it down by noon. Hitched a ride back toward the main road.

When the driver asked where he'd camped, he lied. Said he'd slept in the trees by the glen.

That night, in the hostel, he laid his pack on the floor and found the recorder again.

He didn't remember putting it in there. It was off. The screen black. But when he turned it over, there were scratch marks on the back. Three lines. Almost like the sigil etched into the stone. Not random. Not wear. A mark. Part warning, part memory.

He left it on the windowsill. Didn't touch it again.

By midsummer, a new layer of snowmelt exposed boot prints near the bothy. Just one set. And no one ever came forward to claim the pack inside. Locals stopped talking about it.

But the hill remembered. It always did.

The radio hissed once. Then again. Then silence.

Mara stared out at the ridge.

In the window, her reflection stared back. Only. It wasn't her. Not entirely. Her face was too smooth. Too calm. The eyes wrong.

She stepped back. On the floor below the sill, dust gathered around a boot print that wasn't hers.

In the recorder's static, one word emerged.

Filed.

Then the battery died.

Subject KIN-04

Retrieved tape contains pre-looped segments consistent with Type II breach.

Recommendation: Site containment pending Witness extraction…

Epilogue

Transmission

Dr. Lukas Nygaard sifted through the last of the week's mail with little interest. Bills, two grant rejections, and a flyer for a symposium he wasn't invited to.

Then he saw it.

A small brown package. No return address. No markings beyond his name, hand-written in ink too sharp, too deliberate.

He opened it cautiously.

Inside: a single photograph. Glossy. Slightly bent.

It showed a stone. Palm-sized. Pale grey, with faint runes spiralling outward from a central gouge. The surface glistened as though wet, despite the photo's obvious age.

There was no caption, but Lukas immediately reached for his reference folder. It looked almost identical to a drawing from a 13th-century Icelandic manuscript he'd flagged months ago *Sögur um sjólífið*, an obscure saga detailing strange lights seen over northern waters and an unnamed artifact dredged from the deep.

He flipped the photo over. The handwriting was different from the letter he'd received months ago. Tighter, more frantic. Scrawled in smudged ink across the back:

The voice was never the weapon.

It was always the doorway.

No signature. No return address. Just the black spiral inked faintly in the bottom corner, like a fingerprint pressed too hard.

Lukas felt his pulse shift.

Below the message, a set of coordinates was scrawled. Not for Scotland.

For Norway.

Southern coast.

Lysefjord.

He stared at the paper.

Then reached for his notes.

The patterns. The objects. The stories. They weren't isolated.

They were connected.

And whatever they'd unearthed in the past… *wasn't finished.*

In Glasgow, the nights stayed loud. Buses. Sirens. Rain. But sometimes, around 2:13 a.m., when the city paused for breath, she'd hear it.

Not a knock. Not a voice.

Just the stillness. The kind that watched. The kind that remembered her name.

Inside, the recorder clicked one last time.

Her voice. Not an echo. Not a playback.

"Some places don't haunt you. They become you."

Author's Note

I wrote *The Black Bothy* out of a love for wild places and the quiet, creeping weight they sometimes carry.

This is a story about isolation, grief, memory, and the stories we leave behind, even when we think no one is listening. It's also about the landscapes of Scotland, which feel ancient in ways we don't always have words for. I've never seen anything move in the fog. But I've looked too long at something in the trees and wondered if it looked back.

During my journey and discovering my love of writing, I lost my mum to COVID. The grief stays with me. Still does. I often pour my darkness into the pages I write. Into Mara's silence, her guilt, the need to understand something that won't explain itself. Writing became a way to sit with those feelings, even when they didn't make sense.

If this story lingered with you, I hope you know that was the point.

And for anyone carrying something they didn't choose.

Aidan

Acknowledgements

This story would not have found its shape without the encouragement and insight of several people.

To my family. Thank you for your belief, your patience, and your unwavering support through every late night and revision.

To the friends who read early drafts and offered honest, thoughtful feedback. Your voices echo in these pages.

To the landscapes of the Scottish Highlands, whose silence and mystery continue to inspire and unsettle me, this story is, in many ways, an offering to you.

And finally, to the readers, thank you for stepping into the bothy, for staying through the storm, and for listening closely. I hope the hills remember you kindly.

Next in the series: The Drowned Fjord

The sea never forgets. It only waits. A grieving archaeologist returns to the Norwegian coast after a shipwreck that claimed everything. But the water has brought something back. Beneath the fjord's surface, something ancient stirs, and memory begins to unravel.